Mr Templeton Finds Himself a Wife

A STANTON LEGACY NOVELLA

M.M. Wakeford

First edition.
978-1-7395071-6-9

www.mw-author.com

Contents

The Stanton Legacy

Interconnected steamy historical romances set in England and America from the 1830s to the 1860s following two generations of the powerful and wealthy Stanton family.

Book 1: The Viscount's Scandalous Affair

An illicit affair set in late regency London between two unlikely lovers whose emotional and bumpy journey into love ends in a happily ever after.

Book 2: The Vixen's Unlikely Marriage

A steamy romance set in Victorian England featuring a marriage of convenience between two unlikely characters, a beautiful vixen and a virtuous clergyman, who nevertheless find themselves falling in love.

Book 3: The Bluestocking's Secrer.t Obsession

A slow-burn but steamy friends-to-lovers romance set in Victorian England and America in the Civil War.

Book 4: The Viscount's Forbidden Love

An MM romance set in Victorian England with plenty of heart, angst and steam—and it does have a happy ending.

Stanton Family Tree

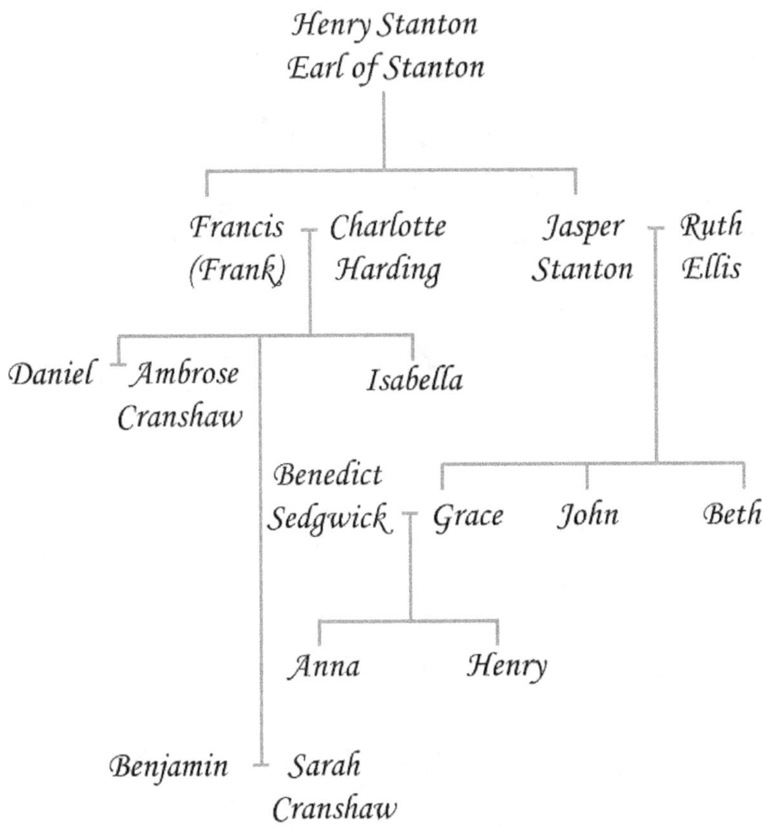

Preface

This historical novella, with spin off characters from <u>The Stanton Legacy</u>, is written for a mature audience. There are graphic sexual scenes that make this story unsuitable for anyone under the age of 18. Although this is a male/female romance, there is one consensual polyamorous scene. If this type of love is not your cup of tea, you have duly been warned.

If you have not read the other books in this series, fear not, as this can also be enjoyed as a standalone novella.

Prologue

Lexie

April 1861

Ambrose's lovemaking had been passionate tonight, even a trifle rough. He had taken her from behind, asking first, "How hard can you take me?"

"As hard as you wish," she had replied.

And with that, her long-time lover had proceeded to drive himself mercilessly into her, his breath hot on the back of her neck. Lovemaking with Ambrose was always a pleasurable affair, but tonight, it had been something startlingly better than usual. She had felt incredibly wanted, as if her lover felt a need to brand her as his possession. For someone long accustomed to being an afterthought to everybody else, having been abandoned by her husband some eight years ago, this was a much needed balm to her soul.

Ambrose Cranshaw had come into Lexie's life first as a kindly neighbour then as a friend. One lonely night nearly a year after her husband, William, had taken off for London, never to return, she and Ambrose had kissed. They had both been a trifle inebriated. One thing had led to another, and from that night, they had become lovers.

Despite finding solace in each other's arms, it was not a passionate affair. Ambrose lived some hours away from Oxford and only came there once a month on business for his employer, Viscount Stanton. On those visits, they spent the night together and made tender love. Over the years, they had come to care greatly for one another, yet something was missing from their relationship. A certain spark perhaps? She could not say. All she knew was that Ambrose was her dearest friend, and one night of every month, her sweet lover too. The rest of the time, she was alone—except for the company of her seven-year-old son, Edwin.

Now, as she came back to reality after a blissful climax, she turned to face Ambrose, whispering, "You are different tonight. What has happened?"

Her lover frowned. "Sometimes," he said slowly, "I feel the need to be strong and dominant. By day, I am compelled to be an obedient servant, but with you, tonight, I wanted to be in command. Did you mind?"

She laughed and kissed his cheek. "I liked it." Pulling back the covers, she got out of the bed. "Let me clean up," she murmured.

Once done, she came back to the bed and into his waiting embrace. She relaxed into his body, feeling content and loved. It was so soothing to be in Ambrose's arms. He had a gentle yet steely quality to him that was wonderfully comforting. She was drifting into a happy reverie, when all at once, her peace was shattered. "It's him. Him that made me different tonight," Ambrose said into the quietness of the night.

Him? What on earth could he mean? She pulled back to look at him. "Viscount Stanton?"

Ambrose nodded.

Frowning in confusion, she asked, "How so?"

Her blood turned to ice at his next words. "From the moment that I met Daniel, I have been subject to strong feelings. It was the same for him, except that while I kept mine hidden, he did not."

He could not be saying what she thought he did. She stared at him, bewildered. "Strong feelings you say. What sort of strong feelings?"

Ambrose held her gaze and uttered the words that broke her heart. "Feelings of desire. Feelings of love."

The horror of her situation began to sink in. Ambrose was in love with someone else—and not just anyone else. Her eyes welled with tears. "You love him," she trembled. "You love a man."

"Yes," he replied succinctly.

She could not stop the sob that escaped her. "What of me? Do you not love me?" she cried.

"Oh Lexie!" He pulled her into his arms and held her tightly, trying to reassure her. "Of course I love you. I always will. You are my dearest friend."

She sank into his embrace, looking for comfort but painfully aware that something precious between them had been lost. Or perhaps it had never been there to start with? They stayed clutched together for several moments in an outpouring of mutual grief. Finally, Lexie pulled away, getting out of the bed to fetch a handkerchief to wipe her face with. She took a deep breath to compose herself. So, Ambrose loved another man, yet he also claimed to love her. What a mess! Once again, she was second best, first with her husband and now with her lover. Perhaps that was the way life was, and she should simply learn to accept reality. Nobody was going to put her first. Only she herself could do so.

Lexie returned to the bed and burrowed back under the covers, sighing resignedly. There was no point in crying over spilt milk. Ambrose may not love her the way she wanted, but he was still her friend. She turned to him. "Tell me," she said.

So, he told her about how he had always had feelings of desire for men and how he had tried in vain to keep them in check. He spoke of his relief when he and Lexie had started their love affair all those years ago—relief at the knowledge he was normal after all, not a freak. But then, he had fallen madly in love with his employer, Daniel Stanton.

They spoke long into the night. When he was done, she asked softly, "What now?"

"We carry on as before," he said.

She pulled back to look at him, full of doubt. "How can we, when it is not me you want but him."

"I cannot have him," Ambrose said softly.

"And am I to be your consolation prize?"

"Never that!" he snapped. Haltingly, he went on to explain, "We are both in the same boat, Lexie. You are stuck in a loveless marriage, abandoned by your spouse, and I live in a world where to display my feelings for Daniel would leave me open to ostracism and possible imprisonment. We cannot change these circumstances we are in, but we can make the best of what we have, which is a deep love and friendship, and yes, desire too. Can you not be happy with that?"

"You propose an affair of convenience then."

"It is more than that, Lexie, and you know it," he told her, then added, kissing her hand, "What I propose is for two dear old friends to provide love and comfort to each other as we have always done. And I promise you this, Lexie. You will always be the only woman for me. Between us there will always be truth. And I will make it my priority to focus on you and only you when were are together like this."

So it was they agreed to continue their affair, as two friends seeking solace in each other's arms. It was not what they truly wanted, but it was something better than being lonely. That night changed things between Ambrose and Lexie in more ways than one. For their lovemaking resulted, nine months later, in a daughter, whom they called Emily.

Over the next few years, Lexie settled into a life as a mother to two young children with an estranged husband living in

London and an occasional lover who came to her bed with tender care, yet loved another man. It was nothing like the life she had anticipated for herself as a girl coming into womanhood. But when did life ever go according to plan? Lexie resigned herself to making the best of it she could.

Chapter 1

Philip

September 1865, four years later

Philip Templeton, pleasure seeker and lover of women, had determined early on in his life—and most particularly on the day he had laid to rest his stern, miserly father—that he would devote his time to the pursuit of happiness. His own happiness, that is. Not for him the dutiful, self-sacrificing life. He had seen enough of that in the twenty years he had lived under his father's thumb.

His deceased parent barely cold in his grave, Philip had made some decisions that were to govern the next two decades of his existence. The first thing he had done was to jettison his studies at Oxford—a double degree in mathematics and theology mandated by his father so that he could at once be inculcated in the righteous knowledge of God's will and develop the numerical skills to manage the substantial fortune that he would one day inherit. Philip had no interest in mathematics nor in theology. What he liked to do was draw and paint, an interest of which his father had actively disapproved. Now, Philip could indulge in his passion for art without hindrance.

However, even at twenty years of age, Philip Templeton was wise enough to realise that a fortune improperly managed could easily be squandered. He had no wish to live in penury later on in life simply because he had been too profligate in his youth. Nevertheless, he was keen to indulge in the things he enjoyed—painting and women.

To resolve this conundrum, he had decided on a simple rule to follow. Thirty per cent of his time would be devoted to the unenjoyable but essential tasks required to maintain his lifestyle. Under this he included scrutinising the accounts, reading the financial section of the newspapers, regular surveys of his property and tenants, exercise—to keep his physique in good shape—and last of all, going to church every Sunday, important to maintain an appearance of respectability.

The remaining seventy per cent of his time he decided would be spent in pleasurable pursuits. This he had done successfully over the years, travelling extensively and painting to his heart's desire, seducing innumerable women and indulging in the most hedonistic of orgies at the exclusive club in London of which he was a dedicated member. Once a month, he took himself to his townhouse in the great metropolis and spent happy hours frequenting Tremayne's, named after the lecherous nobleman who had established it some decades ago. There, he partook of every debauched entertainment imaginable. Then, replete on fine wine and even finer orgasms, he would return to Oxfordshire in time to attend church service on Sunday.

For nearly two decades, this recipe for happiness had stood the test of time—until it hadn't. One evening while at Tremayne's, he had developed an unaccountable disgust for the hedonistic goings on around him and walked out of the club in a dark, perturbed mood. A week had passed in which he could not shake off the gloom that had descended upon him.

And now here he was, back home at Graveley, his Oxfordshire estate, engaged in melancholic musings and unable to muster even a modicum of enthusiasm for the things he had once enjoyed. What was it that had gone wrong with his perfectly ordered life that he was so cast down? Nothing and no one held his interest anymore. Everything seemed dull and lustreless, except for one curious occurrence this week.

He had been riding home from an expedition to Witney, when he had come upon Miss Cranshaw in a state of distress. The eccentric spinster of the village, Miss Sarah Cranshaw distinguished herself by also having harboured an infatuation for him these many years. He could not but be aware of it. She spent church services casting long and adoring glances at him, and blushed in his presence. And despite the fact that Miss Cranshaw was attractive in an unconventional way, Philip had paid her little heed. He had no wish to ever shackle himself in marriage, and seducing innocents was not his way.

But he was a gentleman, and seeing her in distress, he had dismounted his horse and come to her assistance in extricating a young boy who had become ensnared by a man trap in Squire Jonhson's woods. It had felt strangely good to be the hero that day, rescuing a child and earning the gratitude of a fair maiden. He laughed to himself. Strange things indeed had come to pass when the best part of his week was spending time with an upstanding spinster, doing a good deed. Was he turning over a new leaf in his dotage? Questions abounded in his mind over the glum state of affairs he was in, and there was one person he knew who might be able to cast light upon the problem.

"Jenkins," he said briskly, addressing his butler. "Send word to the stable to have Orion saddled."

"Yes, sir," replied the old retainer who had served his family for two decades and more.

Philip donned his boots, coat and hat, then strode down the front steps of his great house to the fine stallion that awaited him, the reins held by a groom.

"Thank you, Walters," he said, taking the reins then mounting his horse. Next moment, he was on his way.

When he arrived at the neighbouring estate of Mulverley Grange, home to Benedict Sedgwick, vicar of his parish, he found it in upheaval, the house servants busy carrying trunks up the stairs. He was about to excuse himself and leave when Benedict appeared, a wailing baby in his arms.

"Mr Templeton," he smiled, over the baby's cries. "What can I do for you?"

"I do apologise, Mr Sedgwick. I can see I have come at an inconvenient time."

"We are packing for our big trip," replied Benedict cheerfully. "We leave for America tomorrow."

"I see. Well, I will not disturb you any further. I do apologise for this unannounced call."

The baby's wails were becoming louder. Really, what noisy, bothersome creatures children were, thought Philip. As if noticing his guest's discomfort, Benedict spoke gently over its cries, "This little one is hungry and needs his mama. If you will wait a few minutes while I take him to her, then we can enjoy a pot of tea with one of cook's freshly baked buns. Do make yourself comfortable in the front parlour, I shall be straight back." So saying, he hurried up the stairs with his squalling progeny.

He was as good as his word, returning a few minutes later, thankfully without any child, followed shortly thereafter by the butler carrying in a tray of refreshments. In the intervening time, Philip had sat in the parlour wondering if it had been a wise decision to come see Benedict Sedgwick, of all people, to discuss his predicament. Once the bustle of pouring the tea and handing out plates had died down, Benedict leaned back in his chair, observing Philip keenly, and asked simply, "What can I do for you, Mr Templeton?"

Philip smiled wryly. "I recall a time some years ago when you came to see me, seeking advice on a matter in which I have a good deal of expertise. Now the shoe is on the other foot, for it is I today, seeking your advice."

Benedict raised a brow in surprise. "You seek advice on a spiritual matter?"

Philip shrugged. "Of a sort. This past week I have experienced a certain malaise in my being, a despondency about myself which I cannot seem to shake."

"I see. Are you aware of anything that might have brought about this despondency?" queried Benedict.

"There was a particular occasion a week ago when I was indulging in one of my pastimes and suddenly found a disgust for it," replied Philip, then adding, "But on further reflection, I believe this despondency has been growing in me for a much longer time."

"This favourite pastime, dare I ask. Was it of a salacious nature?"

Philip's pointed silence was all the answer Benedict required. He frowned. "I am a man of the cloth, Mr Templeton. Surely you must know that my advice will be a renunciation of such evil pastimes and a return to God's way."

"I am well aware of that," Philip smiled sardonically. "However, I am here to speak to you as a man who seems to have achieved that elusive contentment in his life, not as a man of the cloth."

"I'm afraid the two are inseparable," retorted Benedict. "Have you not thought, Mr Templeton, that I may be content because I use the scriptures as my guide?"

Philip blew out an impatient breath. "So you think the solution to my malady is to be found in the scriptures?"

"Undoubtedly so," Benedict said with a laugh. "But if I may, let me start with something the great John Donne, that famous poet and dean of St Paul's Cathedral, once said. *'No man is an island, entire of itself; every man is a piece of the continent, a part of the main.'* Perhaps, Mr Templeton, you have lived too long a life adrift from your fellow man, pursuing your own selfish desires only to realise that such pursuits will not result in a felicitous life."

This was too much. His pursuit of a happy, carefree life was the very thing making him unhappy? What a sacrilegious thing to say! "If you think, Mr Sedgwick," riposted Philip, "that I am about to see the light and embrace a pious, selfless life, then perhaps I was mistaken in coming to see you today."

He picked up his hat and made as if to stand, but was arrested by Benedict's stern command, "Stay." All trace of humour had left Benedict's face as he spoke, "Mr Templeton, you have come to me today seeking my advice, so you will at least have the decency to stay and listen to it in full. I have observed you over the years, sir. You have not involved yourself in local affairs at all, unless it is something related directly to your own business interests. Every few weeks you flit to London where no doubt you indulge in those salacious pastimes we spoke of earlier. You have never courted any gentlewoman with a view to settling down to marriage, yet you have engaged in numerous affairs with women, including, for a short time only, one with my own wife before she had the great foresight of marrying me. I am not unaware of the lifestyle you lead, one which is in thrall to your own selfish desires. And you wonder that you are unhappy? Let me ask you this, Mr Templeton. When was it last that you engaged your time in a matter that related to someone else's wellbeing, not your own?"

Philip had listened to this long speech with an ironic twist to his lips, but now he leaned forward and said derisively, "As a matter of fact, Mr Sedgwick, it was only yesterday that I assisted Miss Cranshaw in the rescue of a young boy who had met with an unfortunate accident. I helped carry him to my horse and took him to Dr Benson. So you see, I am not entirely lacking in selflessness."

Benedict smiled wisely. "I never thought you were, Mr Templeton. So now, let me ask you something else. Was that despondency you have suffered from present in your mind while you were rescuing the boy?"

"I was too busy with the rescuing to dwell on my emotions, Mr Sedgwick," Philip bit back, yet in his mind, he recalled his earlier reflections about this very thing.

"I am sure that you must have experienced some boost to your own wellbeing as a consequence of helping someone else," insisted Benedict.

"Possibly."

"Well, Mr Templeton, I will keep this short, as I do have many pressing matters to deal with before we travel on the morrow. I do not expect you to all of a sudden become reborn as a pious Christian. However, I believe there is merit in pursuing two things over the coming weeks and gauging their effect on your feeling of despondency. First of all, spend a little of your time taking an interest in the welfare of someone other than yourself. You spoke just now of Miss Cranshaw. She does excellent work among the less fortunate in this community, so perhaps you may volunteer your services in assisting her endeavours. Which brings me to the second point. I wonder, Mr Templeton, if it might not be time for you to focus your attention less on women you might seduce and more on gentlewomen you might court with a view to one day finding felicity in marriage. May I once again commend the excellent Miss Cranshaw in that regard, though as a long-standing friend of hers, I reserve judgement as to your worthiness of her."

"Miss Cranshaw?" repeated Philip, with a hint of astonishment. "I have had no thoughts of marriage, Mr

Sedgwick, and none of marriage to Miss Cranshaw, excellent though she might be."

"It was simply a suggestion, Mr Templeton. Make of it what you will. Now, if you will excuse me, I really must be getting back to our travel preparations."

Benedict stood and so too did Mr Templeton, saying, "Mr Sedgwick, I thank you for your time and wish you safe travels."

They walked out of the parlour, towards the main hall. "And I wish you luck in overcoming your despondency, Mr Templeton. Good day."

"Good day." With a bow, Philip took his leave. He rode home in a pensive mood. Once there, he went to his art room and tried to paint, but yet again, inspiration was not to be found. He put the paintbrush down after a few abortive attempts at a still life depiction of objects he had set up on a table. He had no wish to paint them. In frustration, he put on his coat again and went outside for a walk with his dog around the parkland of his estate. The exercise did him good no doubt, but he was still troubled in his mind upon his return. *Damnation!* Was nothing going to lift him from this gloom?

He sat to partake of a light lunch, alone in his study, for he had no wish to sit alone in the great dining room. An insistent voice in his head that sounded suspiciously like Benedict Sedgwick, told him that this was the heart of his troubles. He was alone. And confound it, he did not wish to be alone any longer. So it was that a little while later, he left the house once again, this time riding on his two-seater phaeton. His destination? Ivy Cottage, the home of a certain Miss Sarah Cranshaw.

Chapter 2

Philip

New Year's Day, 1866

Philip set down his empty tumbler and slumped back in his armchair. He was on the way to being well and truly pickled. Who cared? Ever since Sarah Cranshaw had come by to break off the engagement, he had been up in his study, indulging in some fine brandy.

Four months ago, Philip had taken Benedict's advice and spent time with the estimable Sarah Cranshaw. He had been pleasantly surprised to find that not only had he enjoyed her company, but that he was also able to shake off that sense of gloom that had descended upon him. A month later, he had decided to propose. He was nearing forty, after all, and he no longer wanted to be alone and driftless. Marrying Sarah, an attractive and sensible woman who had long held feelings of affection for him, seemed like the perfect solution.

Of course, he had not fallen in love with her, but he had come to care greatly for her beguilingly eccentric ways. Their engagement had proceeded along well, he thought. When they had kissed, he had detected a passionate nature under her prim, spinsterish exterior, all of which boded well for their future union. And then came the thunderclap.

"I have come to see that we would not suit." Those had been Sarah's words to him as she broke off their engagement earlier today. He, Philip Templeton, determined bachelor for so many years and one of the most eligible men in the county, was being jilted. He was going to be a laughing stock, especially after everyone learned that Sarah had cast him aside in order to marry another man. For in her next words, Sarah had confessed her love for Benjamin Stanton.

"I see," he had said in glacial tones. With as much dignity as he could muster, he had promised to send word to *The Times* that their engagement had been called off, then he had haughtily escorted her out.

That was when he had holed himself up in his study with a bottle of brandy. Now, Philip stared glumly into the fire in the hearth. Even in his inebriated state, one thing was clear to him. He had no wish to endure the tittering gossip or pity of local society. First thing tomorrow, he would leave—go to London or even further afield. He would absent himself for several weeks and only return to his Oxfordshire village once all the fuss had died down.

Chapter 3

Lexie

That same day

Lexie sat in her private parlour, the letter that had arrived this morning held loosely in her hand. She supposed she ought to feel a sense of grief over the news that her husband, William Forbes, had passed away after contracting a violent fever. According to the letter, he had breathed his last breath on the night of 30th December, having taken to his bed the week before.

She was a widow now, free to do with her life as she pleased. Well, not quite. Much depended on the state of William's finances and on the provisions of his will. Her thoughts went to her son, Edwin, who was now eleven years old. How would he take the news that his father had passed? Father and son had not been close. In his entire life, Edwin had seen William only on a handful of occasions. Yet still, it might come as a shock. She would take him aside when he returned from his daily lessons with the local schoolmaster and speak to him.

She picked up the letter again and read. It had been sent by William's solicitor, a Mr Ridley.

Arrangements have been made for Mr Forbes's funeral service and interment at St Peter's Church on Eaton Square, to be held on 3rd January. I have taken the liberty of informing the servants of your impending arrival and to have the house at 11 Upper Belgrave Street made ready for you.

If it is not too much trouble, I would also be grateful for an audience with you in the coming week, at a time of your convenience, to go over the terms of the late Mr Forbes's will. I was called to attend to him on 28th December, when it was clear that his condition was grave, upon which time he dictated and signed an updated testament, which was duly witnessed.

Lexie put the letter down and sighed. She would need to travel to London on the morrow. The children would come too. There was no knowing how long she would need to be in London to settle William's affairs, and she could not leave them in the care of the servants. She briefly considered taking them to her parents but dismissed the idea.

Relations with her father had been strained ever since he had learned that William Forbes had seduced her and left her with child. Foaming with fury, he had gone to confront William and insist on a marriage. William, a young man of twenty at the time, had been powerless to resist her father's rage, and the wedding had duly taken place a week later. But once the deed had been done, both men had in their own way shown their displeasure. As soon as he could, William had turned his back on her and gone to live in London. Her father had maintained a cool, distant demeanour with her, which had never regained any warmth. Her mother was more kindly but had to follow her husband's lead. This had left Lexie feeling alone and friendless, but for Ambrose.

Ambrose. She would need to write to him and let him know this new development, though poor Ambrose had troubles of his own. Things had come to a head between himself and the man he loved, Daniel, Viscount Stanton. The long and short of it was that Daniel had left for America some months ago, leaving Ambrose bereft and heartbroken. That had been the impetus, finally, for Ambrose and Lexie to end their love affair and revert to simply being friends. And though they might no longer be lovers, their affection for each other was enduring. Ambrose should be told of William's death, and he would have sound advice, she was sure, on what to do next. Going to her desk in the corner of the room, Lexie took out a blank sheet of paper and began to write to her friend.

Next morning at ten o'clock, dressed in her widow's weeds, Lexie awaited the London train on platform 1 of Oxford Station, together with her son, daughter and Fanny, her maid. Next to them were two large travel cases with their belongings—Lexie had packed for an extended stay, unsure how long they would need to remain in London.

The platform was busy on this Tuesday morning, with many travellers returning to the great metropolis after having spent the Christmas holiday with family in Oxfordshire. Lexie held her young daughter, Emily, firmly with one hand. In the other, she clutched the tickets for their journey. She had been fortunate to reserve the final remaining First Class compartment on the train.

At last, the train chugged into the station with a billow of steam that had Emily jumping up and down in delight. Immediately, there was hubbub as carriage doors were opened and people busied themselves with the business of loading their cases onto the train and finding their seats. Lexie checked the details on the ticket and led her family towards the required carriage. A helpful porter took their luggage and then, with a surge of trepidation, for Lexie had rarely travelled further than a few miles from Oxford in her entire life, they boarded the train.

She pressed down the handle for compartment E, which was the one designated on her ticket reservation, and smiled at an excitable Emily, calling out cheerfully, "Here we go!" With a swish of her voluminous skirt, she entered the carriage only to come to a startled stop. For there, inside her reserved compartment, sat a gentleman idly reading a newspaper.

"Sir!" she blurted, unable to formulate any more coherent words, such was her surprise.

The gentleman lowered the paper and raised a haughty brow. That gesture was enough to make Lexie recover her wits. "Sir," she repeated. "I believe you are in the wrong compartment, for this one is reserved for myself and my family."

"If you check your ticket, madam," he replied coldly, "I believe you will find that it is you that is in the wrong compartment."

Annoyance surging in her breast, Lexie raised her ticket and read out loud, "Reservation on Compartment E, First Class, Oxford to London, departing 10:05, 2nd January 1866. In what way would I be incorrect, sir?"

Now the gentleman stood, irritation evident on his face. He pulled out from his breast pocket an identical looking ticket and stepped towards her, holding it out. She took it from his outstretched hand, placing her own ticket into it for his perusal. Quickly, she studied the ticket he had given her. It too was a reservation for the same compartment, on the same date and departure time. Glancing back up at him uncertainly, she said, "It seems we have both been booked on the same compartment. How can that be?"

By now, the gentleman had finished perusing her ticket. "A mistake by the booking clerk, no doubt," he bit out in frustration. "May I suggest, madam, that you speak to the train guard to see if there is an alternative compartment available for you," he said.

Lexie was not about to go traipsing after the train guard with two children in tow. She had every right to be in this compartment. Why was it not him to go ask about alternative accommodation? Taking back her own ticket and returning his, she said tartly, "I believe I saw the train guard pass by just now. If you are quick, sir, you may find him yourself and discuss the matter." With that, she ushered her children and maid into the compartment and reached for the basket above the seat to place a small bandbox there, which contained sandwiches and drinks for their journey.

The gentleman gave her a sour look, then huffed and strode out of the compartment. Feeling a small sense of victory, she proceeded to settle herself and her family in their seats. "Why was that man so rude?" asked Edwin, coming to sit beside her while Emily came to perch herself on her mama's lap.

Lexie embraced her daughter comfortingly and replied, "No doubt he did not like having his peace and quiet disrupted, but we can hardly be blamed for a ticket clerk's error."

Some minutes elapsed before the gentleman was back, the guard accompanying him. She was asked for her ticket once more. After a cursory examination of it, the guard addressed her with, "I am very sorry, madam. There seems to have been a mix up, and the ticket office erroneously issued two reservations for the same compartment."

"That much is clear. The question is, sir, what can you do about it?" asked Lexie pertly.

"I am afraid, madam," said the guard, "that not much can be done at this late stage. The First Class carriages are fully booked. However, a new booking could be arranged for you on a later train."

"I do not see why I should be made to take a later train when the error was not mine," replied Lexie with asperity. "Indeed, sir, I have two young children with me who will not be amenable to waiting several hours and the consequent delay to our arrival in London. Perhaps the gentleman may be persuaded to wait for the next train."

At this, the gentleman scowled. "I cannot," he stated firmly.

"Then there is nothing for it than for the both of you to share this compartment," concluded the guard. "It seats six persons, and in total there are only five of you, so I am sure you should be comfortable on your journey."

"Cannot the gentleman share a different compartment, one that does not have a lone lady such as myself in it?" protested Lexie, not at all happy with the idea of spending the journey in the company of that ill-tempered man. Said man raised an ironic brow, but the guard was first to speak.

"I am sorry to say, madam, that the train is full, with not a single spare seat in this nor the next carriage. If this arrangement is unacceptable to yourself, then the only thing I can suggest is to wait for a later train."

That idea was insupportable. Already, she was wishing this journey over. She had not slept well last night, beset by worries about the future and what the contents of William's will portended. Perhaps this explained the lack of her usual grace and good humour as she muttered, "Very well, sir, we will share the compartment."

Looking relieved, the guard took his leave, and the gentleman returned to the seat he had vacated a few minutes earlier. With a perfunctory nod, he took up the newspaper he had been reading before and buried his head behind it.

A moment later, the train gave a loud chuff and began to move slowly out of the station. Emily bounced eagerly in Lexie's lap, her eyes glued to the window as she watched the city ebb from view. Soon, they were chugging along through endless green fields, and with the weight of her four-year-old daughter becoming too heavy for comfort, Lexie stood and gently deposited her in the seat by the window, moving to the far corner by the carriage door.

"How long till we get there, Mama?" wondered Edwin.

"Another two hours, I think."

"Will there be someone waiting for us at the station?" continued Edwin with his questioning.

Lexie shook her head with a smile. "I'm afraid not, darling. There was not enough time to write back and let the servants know when our train arrives." She went on reassuringly, "However, they are expecting us today, so you can be sure that there will be a comfortable room and a warm dinner awaiting us."

Edwin was still not satisfied. "What about the family? Will there be any of our relatives there for the funeral, Mama?"

Lexie paused and considered the matter. She had broken the news of William's passing to Edwin yesterday, and he had taken it calmly enough, though he had had many questions about what was to become of them. She had tried the best she could to answer him, but there were many similar questions in her mind too which had yet to be resolved. Over the years, she had had very little contact with the few remaining members of William's family, most of whom had maintained a hostile attitude towards her for the way they believed she had ensnared William into marriage.

"I am not sure, darling," she replied carefully. "Your aunt Christabel lives in Yorkshire with her husband and family, and I do not know whether she will make the journey to London. However, your aunt Cecily should be in attendance, as I believe she and her husband reside in a Kent village not far from London. As I have not been in touch with them, I cannot say for certain."

"What is Aunt Cecily like, Mama?" enquired Edwin, persistent in his quest for further knowledge about his elusive family.

She hesitated, looking out of the window for a tactful answer. The truth was that the one time she had met Cecily

Davenport, formerly Cecily Forbes, that lady had been snooty and obnoxious, looking down her long nose at her. As Lexie returned her gaze to Edwin, her eyes happened to cross paths with the gentleman seated diagonally opposite her. She had not taken much notice of his appearance so far, so it was with a start that she perceived eyes of the brightest blue staring at her from a roguishly handsome face. A tremor of desire passed through her in that instant. Resolutely, she looked away and addressed her son, "Aunt Cecily is several years older than your father, and perhaps because of that, set in her ways, a little like your grandfather."

"If she is anything like Grandfather, then she must be mean," pronounced her son.

"Edwin! How can you talk so?" expostulated a frazzled Lexie, all too aware that the gentleman across from her had lowered his newspaper and appeared to be listening to their conversation.

"Well, but he is," insisted Edwin. "He never smiles nor says a kind word. And he is forever chiding you about this or that. I say that makes him mean."

There was no longer any pretence from the gentleman, who was now watching her with rapt attention. Lexie felt the blood rush to her face, which by its complexion already had a tendency to bloom pink. If only the ground could swallow her whole! Putting on a stern expression, she remonstrated with her son. "Edwin, that is not the way to speak of your elders and you know it. Now let us cease this conversation for it is fast giving me a headache."

She sat back in her seat and closed her eyes, wanting some respite from her children. It was to be short-lived. Not a minute later, she felt a tug on her arm. "Ma, I'm thirsty," complained Emily.

With a sigh, Lexie stood and reached for the band box, opening it to take out the bottle of lemonade in there and a carefully wrapped cup. She poured a measure of the drink and passed it to her daughter. "Hold it with both hands, Emily," she admonished.

The young girl did as she was bid, drinking thirstily. "May I have some more?" she asked.

Lexie tightened her lips. "If you drink too much, Emily, you will need the potty and there is none to be had on this train."

"Just a little bit more, please?" whined her daughter.

Lexie relented and poured another, very small, measure into the cup. "Very well," she said, "but that will be all until we get to our destination or until we are able to avail ourselves of the facilities at the next station."

Emily duly drank the contents of her cup then handed it back to her mama. "May I have something to eat?" she now asked. Edwin too added his voice to this request.

Lexie took out the sandwiches that had been wrapped in a napkin and handed one to each of her children. Next, she invited Fanny, who was a shy, retiring sort of girl, to have some too. "Thank you, ma'am," Fanny said quietly, taking a sandwich and the proffered cup of lemonade.

As Lexie went to help herself to a sandwich, she paused. It would seem only good manners to offer the lone gentleman some refreshment. He had by now retired back to his newspaper. Resolutely, Lexie addressed him, "Sir, excuse me. Sir?"

The newspaper was lowered with a snap, and the gentleman eyed her with annoyance. Gathering her courage, Lexie asked, "May I offer you a sandwich?"

"No, thank you," he replied, then added by way of explanation, "I do not eat between meals."

"I see. Then perhaps you may accept a drink of lemonade."

The gentleman took a moment to consider the matter, then nodded curtly. "Thank you, that is most kind," he said, then took from her the cup of lemonade she had poured and drank it quickly.

As he made to return the cup, something made her say, "Sir, I have not yet had the privilege of making your acquaintance. May I know who it is I am addressing?"

He looked at her in surprise but said readily enough, "Philip Templeton, at your service, madam." He paused a fraction of a second, then enquired in turn, "And who do I have the privilege of addressing?"

"I am Alexandra Forbes," replied Lexie.

"Forbes?" frowned Mr Templeton. "Are you by any chance related to William Forbes?"

"He is my husband, or was—he sadly passed away three days ago. We are on our way to London for the funeral service."

A look of consternation came over Templeton's face. "My God!" he exclaimed. "How did this come to pass? Why only two weeks ago we dined together at White's."

"As far as I know, it was a sudden illness, a fever, that made him take to his bed a week ago," explained Lexie.

Mr Templeton stared at her in shock. "I—I am most sorry to hear it," he said shakily. "Please, Mrs Forbes, accept my deepest condolences."

"Thank you, sir," responded Lexie quietly. "I take it you knew William well?"

"We were acquainted," he murmured. Bowing his head, he took a deep breath, then lifted his eyes to hers. "I suppose one could say we were friends," he said grimly.

They sat back in ponderous silence for the remainder of the time until the train pulled into Reading station. Getting to her feet, Lexie took Emily by the hand, saying to Edwin, "I shall take your sister out to do her business while the train stops here. Do you need to go too?"

At his nod, she turned to her maid. "Fanny, we shall not be gone long, but please stand by the carriage door and make sure the train does not leave without us."

Before Fanny had a chance to respond, Mr Templeton stood, declaring, "Have no fear, Mrs Forbes. I will keep watch until your return."

"Thank you, sir," she replied with an inclination of her head, then quickly escorted her children out of the carriage. They walked along the platform until they found a porter and asked for directions to the lavatories. The way was pointed out to them and soon, they had availed themselves of these facilities. Once they were done, Lexie chivvied her children. "Quickly now," she said, not wanting to hold up the train.

They hurried towards their carriage, where Mr Templeton stood, watching out for their return. He held the carriage door for them as they boarded the train once more. "Thank you, Mr Templeton," said Lexie breathlessly. "That was most kind."

"Not at all," demurred that gentleman.

They resumed their seats in the carriage, just as the train began to move again. The rest of the journey was accomplished in thoughtful, if companiable silence. As the train slowed on its arrival into Paddington station, Mr Templeton roused himself to speak. "Mrs Forbes," he said, "if you will allow me, I would be honoured to procure a hansom carriage and escort you to your home on Upper Belgrave Street."

"That is very kind, sir," smiled Lexie. "However, we would not wish to trouble you to that extent. Perhaps you may assist us in the procuring of the carriage, and we may make our own way to the house."

"It is no trouble at all," responded Mr Templeton, "as my own house is only a short distance from yours."

Lexie did not argue further, acquiescing with grace to Mr Templeton's suggestion. Perhaps she had been unduly harsh in her initial judgement of him. At any rate, she was grateful for his assistance, for she had never before been to London and had been nervous about what to do once they reached their destination.

A short time later, they disembarked the train and were ushered to a line of waiting carriages by the ever solicitous Mr Templeton. Over the course of the journey to Upper Belgrave Street, he engaged Lexie in light and easy conversation. Upon further discourse, she could not help but notice how extremely handsome he was, particularly when he smiled. Not that any of it mattered, she reminded herself sternly. She was a widow in mourning, and not about to engage in a flirtation with any gentleman, no matter how handsome. Still, she could not help a slight flutter of appreciation as Mr Templeton assisted her out of the carriage and escorted her to the house before taking his leave.

Chapter 4

Philip

Philip returned to the waiting carriage after he had seen Mrs Forbes and her family to their door. He instructed the coachman with his address on Eaton Square, then climbed inside the vehicle. It was a short journey to his house — for he had not been exaggerating when he told Mrs Forbes that he lived only a short distance from hers.

Once he reached his home, he alighted from the cab and paid the driver handsomely. His case was brought down and taken inside by one of his footmen while Philip bounded up the stairs to his room to refresh himself after his journey. As he washed his face and hands, he reflected on the events of the morning.

He had been surly, he knew, and nothing like his usual personable self when Mrs Forbes had entered the train carriage with her children and maid. In his defence, his head had been pounding from the after effects of yesterday's inebriation, and his feelings still raw from being jilted by his fiancée. All he had wanted was some blessed peace and quiet, but instead, he had been forced to share the compartment with strangers.

He had tried to stay aloof by hiding behind the large pages of his newspaper. Eventually though, curiosity had drawn him out as he listened to the conversation between mother and son about some funeral they were attending, a distant aunt and a mean grandfather. He had secretly applauded the boy's frank speech about the latter. Mrs Forbes's father sounded like a miserable old goat.

And then he had learned of William Forbes's sudden passing. It had been a shock. While he did not count William as a close friend, he had been on friendly terms with the man. They were both members of White's and their London houses were close by, which meant they often frequented one another. There was one other point of commonality between them, not widely known. For many years, they had both been members of Tremayne's, that secret den of sexual iniquity.

Philip had known, of course, that William was married and estranged from his wife. Not once though, in all the years of their acquaintance, had this wife ever been seen in London with William, to the extent that Philip had almost forgotten the fact of her existence, treating his friend as a fellow bachelor. There had only been one time when William had spoken of her, and that had been four or five years ago, when he had had to cry off a card game on the excuse of having been summoned to Oxford by his wife on some urgent matter.

Of the existence of children, Philip had not been aware. William had never spoken of his son and daughter, which was odd. It was one thing to be estranged from a spouse and quite another to never see one's own children—unless, that is, the children were not his own but by-blows. Philip narrowed his eyes as he gazed unseeing at his reflection in the mirror. In his mind, he examined this possibility. Mrs Forbes had given every appearance of being modest and respectable. He recalled the doe-like brown eyes filled with kindly warmth as she spoke to her children and maid. Those were not the eyes of a wanton seductress. Moreover, she had blushed to the roots of her hair when she had noticed him eavesdropping on her conversation with her son. No, it did not seem to him very likely that this woman had taken lovers and procreated with them at William's expense. But there again the children…

Neither of them had a look of William. The boy bore a great resemblance to his mother, with the same dark hair, rosy complexion and brown eyes, nothing like William's hazel orbs and light brown mane. The girl, on the other hand, showed neither resemblance to her mother nor her father. Golden locks of hair had framed her charming little face, which had stared at him with curious grey eyes. She had reminded him of someone, but he could not for the life of him recall whom it was. *Curious.*

Philip stepped back from the mirror and made for the door, giving himself a mental shrug. At the end of the day, none of this was his business. He was sorry to have been uncivil with Mrs Forbes on their first meeting, but he hoped he had somewhat redeemed his lack of gentlemanly manners in the latter part of their encounter. In any case, he was unlikely to run into William's widow again, except for the funeral, at which he would pay his respects. For the rest of it, she was none of his concern. He had other, more pressing matters, to think about. With this last thought, he strode briskly to his study, where he sat down and wrote a missive to *The Times*, with a request to publish a notice of the termination of his engagement to Miss Sarah Cranshaw.

Once that was done, he went down to the dining room to partake of lunch, sitting down to a meal alone, once again. His spirits took another dive. He was back to the dismal state he had been in not four months ago. What good had been his attempt at reforming his character and settling down to marriage? Nothing had come of it. Perhaps he should give up on the whole idea and go back to the hedonistic life he had led before.

No, that was not the solution to his problem. Had he not grown tired of the endless merriment? The truth was, he wanted a wife, a companion to make this life he led a little less dreary. And perhaps too, he needed a sense of purpose. He had been inspired of late to paint a series of pictures documenting transport through the ages. He still had several paintings to complete in this series, which should keep him occupied. As to the matter of a wife, he supposed eventually he would need to venture out into society and meet eligible ladies for that purpose.

The prospect made him shudder. He had evaded the marriage mart for decades and run far from the simpering misses looking to catch themselves a husband. What irony if he were now to change course and court their attention. He huffed out a long breath. There was no need to rush into it. The season would not begin until spring came around. In the meantime, he would live a quiet life here in his London home and spend his days painting.

Chapter 5

Lexie

The funeral service was finally over. It had not been a large gathering, but there had been several of William's London friends in attendance, including Mr Templeton. Also present was William's sister, Cecily, who was no friendlier on second acquaintance than on the first. Lexie had borne the withering looks and disparaging comments with as good a grace as she could. She was glad, however, that the ordeal was over.

Today, she faced the next challenge—the reading of William's will. Mr Ridley was due to arrive at eleven o'clock, which was any minute now. Lexie sat in the drawing room, waiting anxiously for him. Also present were Cecily Davenport and her husband, which would explain the glacial atmosphere in the room. There was no conversation, only heavy silence and disdainful glances. At last, Lexie heard the welcome chimes of the doorbell, then a male voice speaking to the butler. A moment later, the door opened and Mr Templeton was announced.

Lexie rose to her feet in confusion as the gentleman strode into the room towards her. "Mr Templeton," she murmured. "Good day to you. This is indeed a surprise."

Mr Templeton bowed grimly, then spoke, "Good day, Mrs Forbes. It is indeed a surprise for me too. I received a summons late yesterday evening from Mr Ridley, requesting my attendance here today."

There was a snort from the other end of the room which alerted Mr Templeton to the presence of the Davenports. He bowed coolly in their direction, then came to sit beside Lexie. "Mrs Forbes," he said with great civility. "I hope today finds you well."

"As well as can be, sir, in these circumstances."

"Yes, I quite understand. May I say that I found the service yesterday very uplifting and moving," he went on. "I believe William would have been pleased with the send-off he received."

"I hope so," murmured Lexie.

"And may I also add that several of my acquaintances were much struck by the dignified manner in which both you and your son comported yourselves during the service. I know the circumstances have not been easy for you, Mrs Forbes, but you bore it well."

A cackle interrupted him. "I see the black widow is getting her clutches into her next victim," goaded Cecily Davenport with an acid look.

Mr Templeton frowned in her direction and began to say, "Madam—" but at that very moment, the door swung open and in walked Mr Ridley.

All conversation ceased instantly as the lawyer came into the room and made his bows. In his hand was an official looking leather document case. With great punctiliousness, he took a seat across from Lexie and withdrew several sheets of paper from the case. "I believe it is best I start without any further ado with the reading of Mr William Forbes's last will and testament," he said. "This will was signed by the late Mr Forbes two days before his passing last week. Although he was gravely ill, I can assure you he was of sound mind at the time of the drawing up of this will, which was signed and properly witnessed. In my legal opinion, this document is incontestable and watertight."

He paused, as if waiting for a response from Lexie. Speaking softly, she said, "I am sure it must be, Mr Ridley. Please do go ahead and tell us what is in the will."

"Yes, of course." The lawyer cleared his throat and began to read. "I, William Huntley Forbes, of 11 Upper Belgrave Street, London, being of sound mind, declare this to be my last will and testament, hereby revoking all prior wills and codicils made by me." Mr Ridley continued with the legal preambles until he reached the bequests, starting with some legacies to William's faithful servants. Once this was out of the way, he came to the main part of the bequests. "To my wife, Alexandra Forbes, I bequeath my house at 24 St Michael's Street in Oxford, together with an annuity of £200 for the remainder of her life or until such time as she marries."

"Well, that is excessively generous!" exclaimed Cecily.

She was met with a severe look from Mr Ridley. "If I may finish reading without interruption, madam, that would be appreciated," he stated coolly.

At her disdainful nod, he went on, "To my son, Edwin Forbes, I bequeath the remainder of my assets, including my house on Upper Belgrave Street in London, the Forbes estate at Chevening in Kent, as well as my investments and funds held at Barings Bank. Until he reaches his majority, these assets are to be managed on Edwin's behalf by the following joint trustees: my wife, Alexandra Forbes and my friend, Philip Templeton of Graveley manor in Oxfordshire. I also wish to appoint said trustees as joint guardians to both my children, Edwin and Emily Forbes, until such time as they reach the age of majority."

There were several gasps of surprise at this, not least from Lexie. Mr Templeton was to be a guardian to her children?

Good God why? That question was soon answered by Mr Ridley as he continued reading the will, "Although my wife has been an exemplary parent, I would wish my children, who are still very young, to have the guidance and protection of a gentleman of good standing. I can think of no better person for this task than my good friend, Philip Templeton, whose excellence of character has long been known to me."

"Madness!" exclaimed Mr Templeton. "He cannot in sound mind have thought that I would make a suitable guardian for young children. This is beyond preposterous."

Now it was Mr Templeton's turn to receive a severe look from Mr Ridley. "As I have already assured you," that gentleman now said, "there can be no doubt as to the soundness of Mr Forbes's mind on the writing of this will. I have several witnesses that can attest to it. And as I said before, there can be no contesting of the terms of this will."

"But I cannot in good conscience take on the role of guardian to William's children," protested Mr Templeton.

"I am afraid you must. Should you wish to recuse yourself from the role, then you would need to go through a lengthy legal process in order to do so. As far as the law of this realm is concerned, you are from this day jointly responsible for the welfare of these young children, sir," replied Mr Ridley coldly.

Still Mr Templeton shook his head, repeating over and over, "This is madness."

Lexie sat frozen in shock. She still could not fathom why William would appoint a guardian to her children, one moreover who was a stranger to them all. Was it a cunning plan to strip Ambrose of any rights he might have claimed with regards to the children? What did she know of Mr Templeton, apart from the fact that he was a friend of her late husband and that he was too handsome for his own good?

In a daze, she watched Mr Ridley pack up his documents once more into the leather case. This action seemed to finally galvanise her from her frozen state. In agitation, she addressed the lawyer, "Mr Ridley, pardon me. I have nothing against Mr Templeton, and I am sure he is an estimable man of good character. The fact remains that he is a stranger both to myself and my children. It does not seem right, you will agree, for a stranger from outside the family to be made guardian to my children."

In this argument, she was surprisingly joined by Cecily Davenport. "Sir," that lady snapped, "you say that my brother was in sound mind when he signed this will, but the terms of it are clearly unreasonable. If anyone should be a trustee and guardian of the children, it should be their flesh and blood and not some stranger."

Lexie nodded vigorously to this until she heard Cecily's next words, "In point of fact, the most obvious choice for trustee and guardian of the children should be myself or my husband. As the most senior members of the family, it is only right that we should be placed in such a role."

Mr Ridley merely shrugged then turned to Lexie. "Mrs Forbes," he said, "you have my utmost sympathy, however, the law is the law. Mr Templeton is legally the children's guardian from today, jointly with yourself. May I suggest you spend the next few days acquainting yourself with the gentleman and discussing the main terms of the guardianship, such as where you will set up residence with the children and how often Mr Templeton is to visit to check on their welfare."

He stood, saying with finality, "I shall be on my way now to file this document with the courts. Should you or Mr Templeton have any further queries, then please do not hesitate to write to me on the matter." With that, he made his bows and took his leave.

Mr Templeton too got to his feet. His lips set in a thin line, he bowed to Lexie. "Mrs Forbes, I too shall take my leave. This has obviously come as a shock to us all and shall require much thought. Will you allow me to call on you on the morrow? We shall then, I hope, be in a fitter state of mind to discuss this matter."

"Very well, sir," said Lexie helplessly. She looked to Cecily, whose expression was thunderous. She did not at all wish to be left alone in that lady's company.

As if sensing her discomfort, Mr Templeton turned to the Davenports, addressing them in chilling tones. "Sir, madam, I believe it would behove us to leave Mrs Forbes to reflect on this matter in peace, and I am sure she will need to see to her children. Let us all now take our leave."

He stood, waiting for them expectantly, making it clear that he would not leave until they did. With an irritated huff, Cecily came to her feet, followed like a shadow by her submissively quiet husband. With a stiff nod in Lexie's direction, she bit out, "Good day, madam," and swept out of the room.

Mr Templeton followed suit, pausing at the door to give Lexie one final nod, then he too was gone. Alone in the drawing room, Lexie sank back into her seat, her pulse pounding rapidly at her temple. "*Oh William,*" she thought. "*What have you done?*" Then, for the first time since learning of her husband's death, she put her face in her hands and wept.

Chapter 6

Philip

Back home, Philip paced his study trying to gather his thoughts. He had sent a message to his own solicitor explaining the situation and seeking clarification on the legalities of the will, not that he thought his lawyer would give him a different answer than Mr Ridley had done. What an absolute mess! William's illness must have interfered with his rational thinking for him to appoint a rake such as himself to be guardian to his children. There were no two ways about it.

Seeing that pacing the room was not bringing about any improvement in his mood, Philip flung himself down on his armchair and closed his eyes, taking deep breaths. So, he had been saddled with the guardianship of two young children, but he was not alone in this. Their mother would see to the major part of their care. He would look in on them once every month, or perhaps once a week if they lived nearby. It would be a quick, simple visit to check all was well with them, nothing that would necessitate a radical change in his own lifestyle. As for the financial side of things, it would be easy enough to dedicate a day each month to go through the accounts and ensure that funds were being properly spent. Having resolved matters to his satisfaction, he went to his art room and soon was absorbed in painting.

Next morning, he presented himself once more at 11 Upper Belgrave Street. He was shown into the drawing room, where Alexandra Forbes joined him a short time later. She addressed him politely, if not effusively. "Good day, Mr Templeton."

"Good day, Mrs Forbes," he said, executing a quick bow. Once they had settled themselves in their seats, he waited for her to speak, but a ponderous silence hung over them instead. He observed the nervous wringing of her hands. They were delicate hands with smooth skin and slender fingers.

"It is ludicrous!"

"It is ridiculous!"

They both spoke at the same time, then halted. With a smile, Philip elaborated, "You are quite right, Mrs Forbes. It is ridiculous that I, a confirmed bachelor with no experience of raising children, should be appointed guardian to yours." He sighed then went on, "However, be that as it may, these are the terms of the will, and we cannot easily change them. I have consulted my own lawyer on the matter, and he echoed Mr Ridley's words of yesterday."

"I see," said Mrs Forbes softly. "In which case, I believe we need to discuss arrangements."

He looked at her bowed head and felt a pang of sympathy. He could not imagine what it had been like for her to bring up two children on her own, estranged from her husband, only to now find a total stranger having an equal say as to their upbringing. "Mrs Forbes," he began. "I have no wish to step into your estimable shoes as a parent. We are both agreed that William's decision to make me a joint guardian was ill thought through. Therefore, let us come to an arrangement which we can both live with."

She sat stiffly, those lovely hands of hers still clutched together in her lap. Finally, she looked up at him, eyes brilliant and sparkling with unshed tears. "Very well, sir," she said. "What is it that you would propose?"

He stroked a thoughtful hand along his jaw, considering. "Firstly, let us establish the matter of your residence. Shall you remain in your Oxford house, or do wish to move to either of the other two residences that have been bequeathed to your son?"

She shook her head vehemently and burst out, "I have no wish to move either to London or Chevening."

"In which case, perhaps we can arrange to have those two houses tenanted, until such time as Edwin is old enough to take charge of his affairs," said Philip equably. "I can have my man of business take care of it."

"Yes," concurred Mrs Forbes. "I think that would be best."

Philip let out a relieved breath. This was going much easier than he had supposed. "Now let us come to the matter of your allowance," he continued. "The annuity granted to you by William is for your own personal expenses. However, it would be necessary to disburse a monthly income for the proper maintenance of your family's comforts and needs. What do you think may be an appropriate sum to disburse to you each month for that purpose?"

Mrs Forbes stared at him in surprise. "I—I have lived these past eleven years on the same annuity, without any additional income from my husband," she murmured. "William was very clear that we were to live on £200 a year, which is what I have done, with some judicious management of my funds."

Philip was horrified. "Do you mean William, who is worth at least six thousand pounds a year, only spent a meagre £200 of it on his family?"

"Yes, that is so," Mrs Forbes confirmed, bowing her head in shame. "I was not aware that William had such an income. He always made it seem as if we were a burden to him."

Philip did not know what to think of his recently departed friend. William had never given the impression of being the miserly, penny-pinching sort, so why would he subject his family to such drastic economies? There could only be one conclusion reached. William had done so on purpose as some act of revenge on his wife, and by extension, on his children. Philip clenched his fists in annoyance. If only William were here now, he would give him a piece of his mind. He had no idea what had occurred between William and his wife to cause this estrangement, nor did he care. No matter what it was, William's wife and children did not deserve such ill treatment.

"From now on, you will receive £3,000 a year," he gritted through his teeth. "And if that is not sufficient for your needs, then we may discuss some additional amount."

"Oh!" cried Mrs Forbes, her eyes round with astonishment. "That is excessively generous."

"It is not," stated Philip coldly. "Now let us move on to other matters. If you are to remain in Oxford, then perhaps I may visit once every month to fulfil my guardian duties. And of course, you may write to me at any time should there be the need. Will that be agreeable to you?"

Mrs Forbes's face was flushed pink. "I—yes, thank you."

Philip got to his feet, eager to be gone now that the most important issues had been agreed upon. "I shall write to Mr Ridley to inform him of these arrangements," he said crisply. "Good day, Mrs Forbes." With a bow, he took his leave.

He walked to his house, anger in each step. He could not say exactly why he was so enraged. Perhaps it was something to do with those doe-like brown eyes that had stared at him in surprise when he had made mention of a monthly income. Damn William and his cruelty! It was insupportable to think that all these years, William had lived a life of luxury while his wife had been reduced to the most stringent of economies. It offended every sense that Philip had of what was right and proper.

Once he reached his home, he went to his study and as promised, wrote to Mr Ridley of the arrangements that had been agreed. This duty discharged, he partook of a light lunch, then went to his art room to paint. His current canvas was a depiction of a lord and his lady travelling in an ancient barouche dating back to the 1760s, which he had sketched on a recent visit to Stamford. However, as he took hold of the paintbrush, he found himself distracted, his mind elsewhere.

Minutes elapsed as he stared into space, recalling an expressive pair of brown eyes. He set down the paintbrush and took out his sketchbook and a pencil. Quickly, he began to draw, pausing every so often to recall more clearly the features of her face—the round, rosy cheeks, small white teeth peeking out as she bit her lip nervously, and of course, those large brown eyes that brimmed with emotion. When he put the sketchbook down sometime later, the portrait of Alexandra Forbes was complete.

He rose and shuffled through the stacks of canvases leaning against the wall, looking to find a blank one. Then, he carefully replaced the painting of the barouche with the blank canvas. Going to the table in the middle of the room which held his paints, Philip set about mixing some brown with red, yellow and a hint of black, trying to recreate the exact shade of brown for her eyes. It took several goes before he was satisfied. And then, he began to paint.

He paused only to light more lamps as it grew dark outside. He continued with his task well into the evening and the night. His servants were accustomed to his habits and left him alone. At last, as the first light of dawn appeared in the sky, he set down his brushes and stepped back to inspect his painting, stretching his arms overhead. Yes, he had captured the essence of Alexandra Forbes—shy and nervous, but also fierce and determined to protect her children. The portrait would need some finishing touches, but the essential part was done.

Tiredly, Philip wiped his hands on a rag, then carefully blew out all the lamps except for one, which he took with him to his bedroom. There, he washed quickly and undressed, falling into bed in exhaustion.

Chapter 7

Lexie

Lexie sat in William's study, a stack of bills on the desk before her. These had been received in the past few days from various tradesmen, looking to be paid for their services. She examined each bill before placing them in a stack to be sent to Mr Templeton for settlement with the bank.

As she looked through each one, she found herself shocked at William's extravagant lifestyle, such as paying the exorbitant sum of £4 for a new hat. She shook her head, vowing never to fall prey to such ridiculous profligacy, even with the great improvement in her financial circumstances.

Eventually she came to a bill written out in elegant script, the name Tremayne's printed at the top. It was for the renewal of William's membership of this club for another six months. She frowned, placing the bill to one side. She would have to write to Tremayne's and inform them of William's passing. They would then understand why the subscription would not be renewed.

A moment later, she picked the bill up again and scrutinised the address printed in the top left corner. If she was not mistaken, the location was very close to this house. Abruptly, she rose and went to a map of London that adorned the far wall of William's study. She traced a finger and found Chester Street. Yes, she had been correct. It was but a five minute walk from here. Better she went in person and dealt with this matter, rather than wait days or weeks to have it sorted out. She hoped to settle all outstanding matters over the next day at most, and then to take her family back home to Oxford.

Decision made, she left the study, the bill tucked into her pocket, and went across the hall to the parlour which was being used by the children for their entertainment. Inside, she found Emily and Edwin busy constructing houses with a set of playing cards. At her entrance, Emily looked up and accidentally nudged a card, sending the house she had been building crashing down. "Oh no!" she cried in frustration.

"It's alright, Emmy," soothed her brother. "We can build it up again."

"Darlings," said Lexie. "I have a quick errand to run. I shall be gone at most half an hour. Make sure you mind what Fanny says while I am gone."

"Yes, Mama," they both echoed.

She smiled, a wave of affection rushing through her. They were good children. Apart from a little fussing last night from Emily, they had endured the past few days uncomplainingly, although she knew they all wished to be back home.

With a smile at Fanny, Lexie left them to their games and went to put on her coat and bonnet. A short while later, she let herself out of the house and began the walk to Chester Street. She looked about her curiously as she walked, still unfamiliar with the hustle and bustle of London.

It did not take long to reach her destination. She rang the bell and waited. Presently, the door was opened by a stern-faced butler. He took in her appearance before asking in implacable tones, "What may I do for you, madam?"

Lexie put on her friendliest smile. She knew from experience that a warm smile went a long way towards thawing people's manner towards her. "Good day, sir," she said courteously. "I am Mrs Forbes, widow of William Forbes, who is a member of this club. I would like to discuss a bill that I received today. I wonder if I could have a short audience with the owner of this establishment."

The butler examined her coolly for several long moments before stepping back and allowing her to enter. "If you will follow me, Mrs Forbes," he said, leading her to a small parlour on the ground floor. It was furnished with simple elegance, comprising a settee and two chairs facing an ornately carved fireplace. "Do take a seat, Mrs Forbes," the butler now said, "and someone will be with you shortly to discuss this bill."

"Thank you, sir," replied Lexie, lowering herself onto one of the chairs. The door shut behind the butler, and she took the ensuing time to examine the room more closely. There was a painting of horse riders in Hyde Park adorning one of the walls and a rich tapestry decorating the opposite side. The place looked like the home of a well-to-do person, and she relaxed a little in the knowledge that she was in a salubrious establishment.

She was busy in contemplation of the tapestry scene when the door slid open and a lady of uncertain age entered the room. Lexie quickly stood in greeting, curtsying politely.

"Mrs Forbes, how do you do?" said the lady. "I am Mrs Barry, owner of Tremayne's."

Lexie's eyes flew to hers in surprise. She had not thought that a lady would be the owner of a gentlemen's club. There again, what did she know of London ways? With a hesitant smile, Lexie returned the greeting, "How do you do, Mrs Barry."

As both ladies took a seat, Mrs Barry enquired, "Now, what can I do for you, Mrs Forbes?"

Lexie took a deep breath, hating this part of the proceedings, where she had to speak of William's passing and accept condolences from strangers. "Mrs Barry," she began, "I am very sorry to say that my husband, William Forbes, sadly passed away just over a week ago."

"Oh, my dear, I am so very sorry to hear this," cried Mrs Barry. "Please do accept my deepest condolences."

"Thank you," replied Lexie graciously. "This morning," she went on, "I received a bill from your establishment for the renewal of the subscription for my late husband's membership. Since he has now passed away, you will of course understand why I cannot settle such a bill."

"I am afraid I understand no such thing," responded Mrs Barry, her tone decreasing in warmth. "We have very particular rules, which each person agrees to when they take out a membership of this establishment. The rules say very clearly that any termination of a subscription must be done at least thirty days prior to the next bill being due. Since Mr Forbes did not inform us within that time, at which he was still living, that he wished to cancel the subscription, then I am afraid it must continue for another six months, and the payment of the bill is due."

Lexie gazed at Mrs Barry in consternation. "Nevertheless," she protested, "I am sure allowances can be made given these sad circumstances. Mr Forbes is not here to partake of the many benefits due to him as a member of this establishment. It would seem unfair, therefore, to be made to pay for services that will not be incurred."

"Mrs Forbes," replied Mrs Barry with an unctuous smile, "as his widow, the membership of Tremayne's passes on to you, and you are now free to partake of such benefits. I am sure that you must be aware of what these entail, are you not?" She raised a brow enquiringly.

Lexie was not about to disclose that her husband had abandoned her without a backward look. With as much dignity as she could muster, she proclaimed falsely, "Of course. My husband often spoke of how much he enjoyed coming to Tremayne's and the many delights to be found here."

"Well then," said Mrs Barry, "you are welcome to come and enjoy such delights, Mrs Forbes—only please do ensure you have settled the bill within a reasonable time."

Lexie bit her lip and tried once more. "I am afraid not, Mrs Barry. I am now in mourning and cannot be going out for entertainment, besides which, I shall shortly be returning to my home in Oxfordshire."

Mrs Barry let out an unbecoming titter. "Oh, Mrs Forbes," she said with a chuckle. "You must know how discreet we are here at Tremayne's. Whether or not you are publicly in mourning is immaterial. You may come and partake of our delightful entertainment with no fear of any gossip being spread in society about it. In fact, why not pay us a visit this evening? I am sure it will do wonders for you in helping to get over your feelings of grief."

Lexie was not sure what these delightful entertainments were—no doubt some diverting music or dancing, perhaps also some culinary delicacies. A part of her yearned to shed the strain and tension of the past few days and to have a few hours of simple pleasure. But she could not go out all alone at night. She said so now to Mrs Barry who laughed again, "Of course, you may do so. Several of our members are ladies such as yourself, Mrs Forbes, who patronise this establishment on their own. Rest assured that you will receive a warm welcome."

"Well in that case," said Lexie tentatively, "I shall pay Tremayne's a visit tonight. What time pray should I arrive?"

"I would advise arriving at eight o'clock, Mrs Forbes," replied Mrs Barry, all good humour now restored.

"Then that is what I shall do." Lexie got to her feet and inclined her head. "I will wish you good day, Mrs Barry."

Chapter 8

Philip

Philip woke late and emerged from his bed feeling groggy, as he often did after an all-night session of painting. His lassitude improved once he had a wash, a shave and a hearty lunch—for breakfast time had already come and gone by then. He decided a walk in the fresh winter air would be just the thing to revive him, and while he was at it, he would call on Mrs Forbes, as a courtesy of course.

A brisk walk later, he presented himself at 11 Upper Belgrave Street, only to be told that Mrs Forbes was out, but that she was due to return shortly. He considered waiting for her, but in the end, thought it best to leave and call another time. He took a further turn around the square and went home, feeling equal parts disappointed and relieved.

Up in his art room, he gazed once more upon the painting he had made of Alexandra Forbes. He had painted her face, brown eyes brimming with troubled emotion, one dainty hand cradling her cheek. He picked up his paintbrush and added a few finishing touches to that delicate hand and to the golden brown curls gathered loosely at her neck. Then, he stepped back and assessed his work.

It was, even to his subjective eyes, one of the finest paintings he had ever crafted. There was subtle beauty in the lady's face, but that was not what called out to him. It was the emotion in her regard, one that evoked an answering reaction in him, for those brown eyes, he realised, held a mirror to his own feelings these many months past—alone, unfulfilled. It was as if he were gazing upon a kindred spirit. Abruptly, he turned away, snickering in self-derision. Kindred spirit indeed! What flight of fancy he was indulging in.

As he closed the art room door behind him, he wondered what he should do with the painting. He did not wish to ever exhibit it, even if it was his finest achievement as a painter. There was about it something too personal to share with the wider world. Neither did he want the painting to be seen by visitors to his house nor for it to moulder away in a hidden cupboard. Upon further reflection, he decided he would take it home with him to Graveley whenever it was that he eventually returned, and that he would hang it in a corner of his dressing room where only his eyes would land upon it each day.

He spent the rest of the afternoon at home, reading and going over some of his accounts. When evening came, he decided he ought to go out and dine at White's. Some company was what he needed to snap him out of this melancholic mood. For a brief instant, he considered giving Tremayne's a visit, a place he had not been to for over four months, but he discarded the idea. The solution to his problems was not to hark back to his old ways; it was to forge a new path. Once the season began, he would mingle and look out for a possible new bride, one that would this time not jilt him close to the altar.

A little before eight, he left his house, dressed for the evening, and hopped into his waiting carriage, instructing the coachman to take him to White's on St James's Street. As the carriage clip clopped on the cobbled streets, Philip gazed out of the window at the houses they passed, faintly illuminated by oil lamps dotted along the way. On passing Upper Belgrave Street, he noticed a person wearing a dark cloak emerge from number eleven. He sharpened his gaze and tried to discern who this person could be. He had very little time to do so, as his carriage quickly overtook the cloaked figure. From the fleeting glance, he saw that it was a woman but could not discover her identity. A servant perhaps?

A moment later, he knocked on the roof of the carriage with his cane, instructing the coachman to stop. Then, watching closely for movement outside his window, he spied the cloaked figure once again as she walked briskly in his direction. Her head was bowed and practically hidden beneath the hood of the cloak. As she passed under a street lamp, however, he was given a brief glimpse of her face. It was Alexandra Forbes.

Where on earth could she be going on her own at night? He sat indecisive in his carriage for a few moments, then came to a decision. Opening the door quietly, he jumped down and bade his coachman return home. He would make his way to his club on foot, despite the coolness of the evening. Then quickly, before he lost sight of her, he set to following Mrs Forbes.

At the corner, she turned right onto Chester Street. Phillip followed at a safe distance. She did not go far. A minute later, she stopped in front of a building well known to him. What the devil was she doing at Tremayne's? He saw her ring the bell and be ushered inside. Without hesitation, he followed suit, entering his old haunt a few moments later.

As the butler took his coat and hat, he enquired casually, "There was a lady just walked in. I believe her to be a Mrs Forbes. Where may I find her?"

"I believe, sir, that she is in the dining lounge," replied the butler.

Philip nodded his thanks and took the stairs two at a time to reach the dining lounge on the first floor. He strode into the lounge, a richly furnished room that contained around a dozen dining tables scattered around the room at a discreet distance from each other. He tracked the room with his gaze until it landed upon Alexandra Forbes, taking a seat at an empty table in the corner. Without thinking, he headed towards her. "Mrs Forbes," he said, taking the seat across the table from her.

She gaped at him in surprise. "Mr Templeton," she mumbled. "I had not known that you too were a member of this club."

Before he could answer, a waiter came to them to take their order. Philip gazed askance at Alexandra. "Will you share a bottle of Claret with me, Mrs Forbes?" he asked.

"Are you come here alone, Mr Templeton, or are you meeting acquaintances of yours?" she said by way of reply. "In which case, I would not wish to inconvenience you."

"I am alone, Mrs Forbes, and I assure you there is no inconvenience," was his quick response.

She smiled shyly. "Then yes, sir, I would be happy to have Claret wine."

Philip looked to the waiter, who nodded in understanding. "Shall you be dining tonight, sir, madam?" the latter now asked.

Lexie's eyes flew to his in inquiry. For an answer, he said lightly, "I would heartily recommend the beef steak with sautéed potatoes."

"Yes, that sounds good. I shall have the beef steak please," she decided, addressing the waiter.

"And me too," Philip added. The waiter nodded and left them then. As soon as he had gone, Philip narrowed his eyes at Alexandra and demanded, "So, Mrs Forbes, do please tell me how you happen to be at this club tonight."

She looked taken aback at the accusatory tone of his voice. "I—well, you see, this morning, I received a bill for the renewal of William's subscription to the club. I saw from the address that it was close to the house, so instead of writing back, I decided to come in person, and that is when I spoke to Mrs Barry, the owner of this establishment."

Philip frowned. "Do go on," he urged her.

"Well, the long and short of it was that Mrs Barry insisted that the bill be paid, even when I explained that William had passed away—something to do with giving notice thirty days beforehand. I did try my best to remonstrate with her about it, but she would have none of it and said the membership had passed on to me and could not be cancelled for another six months."

Philip gazed at her sternly. "I do wish, Mrs Forbes, that you had come to me with this matter. I would have dealt with it on your behalf."

Alexandra's brown eyes flashed momentarily. "I am not so helpless, sir, that I am unable to fend for myself," she said, taking issue with his words.

"This does not explain why you are here tonight," he countered smoothly.

She shrugged uncomfortably. "Mrs Barry said I should come and enjoy the entertainments tonight, and that it would help alleviate my grief. So, since there is no possibility of cancelling the subscription, I thought to come and make use of it. Mrs Barry assured me that it would be quite alright for me to come here alone, even at my time of mourning. This establishment is very discreet, you see."

Philip's lips quirked in amusement. He was well aware why discretion was of the utmost importance to the club. "And what sort of entertainment do you think to enjoy tonight?" he wondered idly.

Alexandra looked about the room. "Well, sir," she confided, "as to that I am not sure. I can see we shall be treated to some fine food, and perhaps some music later on? Also, I have noticed some ladies and gentlemen enter the room beyond." She nodded to the door at the far end of the lounge. "Is it some kind of ballroom where the patrons may indulge in a dance or two?"

Philip sighed internally at Alexandra's innocence. He would have his work cut out tonight, ensuring she did not find out what actually went on in that room. It was not dancing, that was for sure! He thought quickly about how he could fob her off. "No, it is not a ballroom," he said gently. "This club is known for being… how shall I put it? Well, the blunt way to say it is that it is a gambling hell of sorts, where patrons play a variety of card games for very deep stakes. If you will pardon me for saying so, Mrs Forbes, it is not at all the kind of place you should frequent."

"Oh," she said, disappointment evident on her face. "What a shame. I had hopes to enjoy the entertainment tonight." She cast him a hopeful look. "Perhaps we may go in for a short time, only that I may see it."

"No," he stated firmly. "That will not do at all, Mrs Forbes. You shall have to take my word for it."

She looked unconvinced, but fortunately just then, their food arrived, and they were distracted for a while with the business of enjoying their steak and wine. He decided to distract her further by changing the topic of the conversation. "So, tell me, Mrs Forbes," he asked curiously, "how did you first meet William?"

"It was years ago, when he was at Oxford," she replied. "My father is proctor of the college where William was a student. Every Michaelmas, Father hosted a dinner for the students, and that year—I was barely eighteen at the time—I was seated beside William for the meal. I had never attended the Michaelmas dinner in previous years, being deemed too young, so you can well imagine how shy and nervous I was that day. William was charming, putting me at my ease, and I could not help but be entranced by him."

"Yes, he could turn on the charm quite easily," agreed Philip, not at all unaware that this was something that he himself was also guilty of. "So," he prompted, "you both fell in love, and he proposed?"

She flushed, her rosy cheeks going a deep pink. "Umm, it was not quite that way, but we did obviously get married," she prevaricated.

"Mrs Forbes, since we are to share guardianship of your children, I believe we have gone beyond being mere strangers, don't you agree?" enquired Philip.

"Yes, I suppose so."

"In that case, will you not allow us to address each other by our given names? I am Philip, by the way," he smiled at her.

"My friends call me Lexie," she giggled charmingly.

"Lexie." He tried the name out on his tongue. It suited her. "I like it," he said, catching the brief, pleased look on her face. "So, Lexie, we have gone beyond mere acquaintances. Will you tell me why you and William have been estranged all these years?"

She looked down at her plate, taking undue interest in slicing her potatoes. "It is not a very edifying story, I'm afraid," she murmured.

He snorted. "I am hardly a saint, Lexie, so I will not judge, I promise."

She sighed deeply. Then, still not looking at him, said, "I was infatuated, believing myself madly in love with William. Over the next weeks, we met in secret several times, and the result of those encounters was that I became with child."

"I see," he said softly.

"When Father found out, he was enraged," she explained. "He threatened to expel William from the college if he did not do the right thing and marry me. So, within a week, we were wed."

"And I am guessing that William did not take well to this enforced marriage," mused Philip, his eyes glued to her face.

"No, he did not," she concurred. "As soon as Edwin was born, which coincided with his graduation from the college, William was away to London. I only saw him a handful of times after that."

He continued to fix her with his stare. Something did not add up. "And Emily?" he asked gently.

She picked up her wine glass and drank the contents up in one go. When she failed to answer, he did so instead, "She is not William's daughter."

She shook her head.

"Who, may I ask, is the father?"

"It is Ambrose Cranshaw," she said, finally looking up at him.

Now it all made sense. Emily had reminded him of someone, and he realised who it was. "She bears a striking resemblance to him," he said.

"Yes, she does," agreed Lexie. "I suppose, being engaged to Sarah, you have become well acquainted with Ambrose."

Sarah. He had almost forgotten. "We are not engaged anymore," he said abruptly. "She broke it off a few days ago to run after Benjamin Stanton."

"What?" Lexie stared at him in shocked surprise. "I had no knowledge of this."

"I received a letter today from Benedict Sedgwick, the vicar of my parish," went on Philip. "He informed me that Sarah has left for America to marry Benjamin Stanton, and that her brother has gone with her."

"So that is why I have not heard back from Ambrose," cried Lexie, looking upset. "I wrote to him the day I received news of William's passing, and I have been waiting each day for a response from him. America, you say? He could be gone for months." She sniffed and wiped an errant tear, clearly distressed at the news.

Philip's mouth turned down at the edges, a flurry of jealousy swarming through his breast. "Yes, it may be weeks until you see your lover again," he stated flatly.

"We are not lovers, not anymore," she denied. "Our ten-year affair has run its course, and we agreed to being just friends."

He felt relieved and angry at the same time. Ten years his lover? That was a very long time. He did not know why that should make him so mad, but it did. Before he could speak, she added, "It is not for myself that I am upset, although I had wanted to speak with Ambrose about all this that has happened with regards to the will. No, it is for Emily that I cry. We are used to having Ambrose visit us each week in Oxford. Already, she keeps asking when we may see him again. I fear she will take his prolonged absence badly. Edwin too."

"Poor little lass," he commiserated, then went on to ask, "When do you propose to return to Oxford?"

She took a sip from the wine that Philip had replenished in her glass. Setting it down, she said, "I had hopes we could go the day after tomorrow, that is if all the most pressing matters can be attended to by then."

"I do not see why not." He made a quick decision then, overturning his plan to stay away from home and avoid the gossip about his broken engagement. "I shall travel with you to Oxford," he said in a voice that brooked no disagreement. "Leave it with me, and I shall procure the proper tickets and reservations."

She laughed. "That ought to ensure we are not double booked to the same compartment."

"I believe we can call that a most delightful serendipity," he smiled warmly at her.

"You did not look too happy about it at the time," she reminded him with a twinkle in her eyes.

"I was not in the best of humours that day," he said ruefully. "Perhaps now, you may understand why."

She gazed at him in sympathy. "Were you very much in love with Sarah?"

He took a last bite of steak and set down his cutlery. "I was very fond of her and thought she would make an admirable wife, but I was not in love," he admitted.

She nodded in understanding. "There comes a time when one wants to settle down with a life companion, for as the saying goes, no man is an island."

"It is funny you should say that," remarked Philip. "That is exactly what Benedict Sedgwick said to me when I spoke to him about my woes."

"Your woes?" Lexie raised a brow in query.

"It is a long story," Philip demurred. "Suffice it to say, I was feeling melancholic about my life and went to seek advice from my vicar. He told me that for too long, I had lived in thrall to my selfish desires, and that I should take the time to involve myself in the wellbeing of someone other than myself." He laughed shortly. "What would he say now, at the news that I am to be guardian to two young children?"

"And that was when you proposed to Sarah?" wondered Lexie.

"It was a few weeks after that, but in truth, I had been thinking for a long time about settling down." He gave her a sheepish look. "The bachelor life loses its sheen after a while."

They paused their conversation on seeing the waiter return to collect their plates and enquire about the next course. They both agreed to a portion of bread and butter pudding.

Returning to the subject of their conversation, Lexie remarked, "It was quite a shock to me to learn you would become Edwin and Emily's guardian, but on further acquaintance with you, I am becoming more reconciled to the idea. I hope I shall not have cause to change my mind."

He reached across and took her hand in his. The skin was as soft as he had imagined it to be. "Lexie, look at me," he commanded. When she raised her eyes to his, he went on, "I am very aware of the huge honour and responsibility that I now bear with regards to you, Edwin and Emily, and I promise you this. I will do my utmost to care for their welfare as if they were my own children. I mean to take my duty towards them very seriously."

She nodded at this, saying shakily, "Then all shall be well, I hope."

He let go of her hand as the waiter approached with their puddings. They ate these quietly, each lost in their own thoughts. When they were done, he enquired, "Well, Lexie, shall we go?"

"Is there not to be any music?" she asked hopefully.

He hid a smile. "I am afraid not."

"Very well," she said with a sigh. "Let us be on our way."

Philip stood and held out his hand to Lexie. She rose to her feet, patting her skirts down, then placed her hand in his. He led her towards the staircase, congratulating himself on managing this difficult situation with aplomb. But in this, he was too hasty. For just as they were about to leave the dining lounge, they were accosted by a lady and her gentleman. "Philip!" she cried, throwing her arms around his neck. "It has been an age since we saw you here. Please do not say you are leaving. I was hoping we could partake of some fun together."

"Cleo," he said, extricating himself from her arms. "It has been an age, but I am sorry to say, I will not be joining the game tonight."

"The game?" she asked in surprise. Her eyes took in Lexie, standing beside him and listening with avid perplexion to their discourse. "And who is this delightful lady?" she enquired.

Lexie raised her brows haughtily, evidently not used to being addressed with such familiarity. "I am Lexie Forbes," she said, straightening her spine.

Cleo's face fell. "Do not tell me you are William's wife? My dear, I was so sorry to hear the sad news of his passing."

Lexie nodded, mumbling, "Thank you."

Cleo's husband drew her to him then, saying, "Darling, we really must be getting on. I am keen to enter the room of pleasure and get started with our fun."

"Yes, dear," she replied, then looking at back at them, she added, "I hope we may see you here soon, Philip. We have missed you." And with a final smile of farewell, she and her husband moved towards the door at the end of the dining lounge.

Now Lexie turned to him, face fuming. "The room of pleasure?" she taunted. "That does not sound to me like a room for playing card games. What is beyond that door, Philip? Tell me!"

"It is not a room you should be visiting." He tried to lead her once more towards the stairs, but she would have none of it, snatching her arm away.

"Perhaps I may be the best judge of that," she threw at him, already marching towards the door.

He followed close behind, warning, "Lexie, do not do this. Trust me."

She ignored him, quickening her footsteps. Placing her hand on the door handle to the room of pleasure, she cast him one last triumphant glance before opening the door and entering.

He followed her in, bracing himself for what was to come. Inside the room, the light was several shades dimmer than in the lounge, but what was going on in there was still plainly evident. Lexie came to a surprised halt and stared. All around her were naked people in various stages of sexual congress. Her eyes went round as she stared, gasped and stared some more. "What sort of place is this?" she whispered under her breath, but he heard her well enough.

"It is a place where like-minded people go for physical pleasures," he replied softly.

She could not take her eyes off a group that comprised a woman and three men, all of whom were busy pounding their cocks into the woman's orifices. "This is so depraved," she muttered, but still could not look away, and neither could he — not from the sexual games going on around them, but from her. His sharp eyes took note of her shortened breaths and the way her eyes dilated. "*Why, she is aroused by this sight,*" he thought to himself.

Just then, a maid came up to them. "May I undress you, sir," she asked him. He shook his head and dismissed her.

Lexie's attention strayed from the spectacle momentarily. "You come here too and take part in all this, don't you?" she accused.

"Yes, though not for several months. Not while I was engaged to Sarah."

She shook her head disbelievingly. "Why? Why would you do such a thing?"

He stepped closer and whispered into her ear. "Why Lexie? Because it is infinitely arousing and enjoyable to carouse naked with others, to watch another person take their pleasure and to be pleasured in return. I make no apology for it. While I am a bachelor and unattached in any way, such enjoyments do nobody any harm."

He felt her shiver at his words, or was it at the sight she saw? "Some of these people are married, though," she argued.

"Yes, some are, and that is a matter for them to decide. I was speaking only on behalf of myself, as an unmarried man."

Her mind was quickly working out something else. "William came here too, of course. Is that how you met and befriended him?"

He sighed. "I saw him here, yes, but I met him in other, more salubrious circles. Do not forget also that we were near neighbours."

Just then, the woman they were watching cried out, her eyes closing in orgasmic bliss. Shortly thereafter, the man that had his cock in her mouth pulled out the shiny appendage and ejaculated his seed all over her generous breasts. "Oh my," whispered Lexie, quite overcome.

He brought his lips to her ear once more. "Would you like that, Lexie? Would you want a man to shower you with his seed? Claim you as his?"

Her breath hitched at his words, but then it was as if a shutter came down, bringing her back to her senses. "I have seen enough," she gritted, and hurried towards the door.

He followed her, realising too late that his cock was rock hard and jutting out most noticeably in his trousers. He shut the door to the room of pleasure behind him and took a deep breath to try to calm his excited body. Lexie continued on her way, not noticing his predicament. Down the stairs she went, throwing out an imperious command for her cloak and bonnet.

The elderly butler went to fetch both their coats as they waited in the hallway. After a time, Philip was relieved to see that his male appendage was beginning to soften to a more acceptable girth. Not that it mattered, since Lexie was determinedly not looking his way. Finally, they dressed in their outdoor clothing and were ready to leave. He took her arm firmly and led her outside. In the coolness of the night, they walked quietly together, neither of them speaking.

Eventually, Philip broke the silence. "Lexie, what you saw in there was debauched and depraved, but do not judge too harshly those that take joy in such merriment. It is not a place I would have ever willingly taken you to, my dear, and I am sorry you had to see it."

"I am not," she responded softly. "I am not likely to forget in a hurry what I saw tonight."

"Did you like what you saw?" he asked huskily.

"I—I should not, but it was strangely captivating," she breathed.

"Yes, it was," he agreed, thinking back to the sight of her watching and becoming aroused despite herself.

"Are you… do you ever plan to go back there again and take part in that carousing? Now that you are no longer engaged, that is."

He glanced at her stiff profile. "No, I had not planned to do so. My thoughts were to mingle in society once the season begins and to set about finding myself a wife."

"I see." She sounded almost disappointed. *How interesting*.

"Well," she added, "I have learned much in this visit to London, but I think I am more than ready to return home." By now, they had reached her door at 11 Upper Belgrave Street.

"Then home is where we shall go," he reassured her. "Goodnight, Lexie."

"Goodnight, Philip."

After a quick nod in his direction, she walked up the steps and knocked on the door, which was opened by the butler. Philip watched her disappear inside, then turned and headed towards his own home, deep in thought.

Chapter 9

Lexie

Lexie lay in her bed, unable to sleep. What she had seen tonight was unimaginable. Wicked. Depraved. She had never thought that people could behave like this. And yet part of her was unabashedly curious about the goings on at Tremayne's. What must it be like, she wondered, to shed all societal and moral precepts, and to behave with such wanton abandon? When she had asked Philip if he planned to return there, she had half hoped he would say yes, and then she would have begged to accompany him. Madness!

She tossed in her bed racked by images of what she had seen and by sinful imaginings. In her mind, she saw herself going to Tremayne's with Philip and shedding her clothes. She would get to see him unclothed too and finally cast eyes on the large bulge she had spied, very briefly, in his trousers. Then what would they do? Here, her imagination took an even more wicked turn. What if she were to lave Philip's cock with her tongue while a stranger took her from behind? Oh my!

With each thrust of that stranger inside her cunt, Philip's cock would plunge deeper into her mouth. She would feel the satin of his skin and taste the saltiness of his spend. Lexie had pleasured a man's cock before, of course. Over the years, she and Ambrose had experimented with different variations to their sexual congress. She had enjoyed the act of licking his cock, both for the taste and sensation, but also for the power it gave her to give pleasure. Each time, Ambrose had cried hoarsely, his control gone, as he spent into her mouth.

In her mind's eye, she saw herself sucking vigorously on Philip's great cock, making him lose all self-control too. And as the stranger behind her continued thrusting into her, Philip would climax, not in her mouth, but over her breasts, painting her with his seed. She shivered deliciously at the thought. Her hand crept down to touch her core and found it dripping with her arousal. It took only a few rubs of her questing fingers to reach her own quiet climax.

Afterwards, she lay breathless in her bed, slowly emerging from the haze of her fevered dream. That was all it could be—a dream. For in reality, she could never behave as those wanton revellers had done this evening. It was a good thing that they were to return to Oxford soon, and she could begin to put this madness behind her. But could she likewise put a lid on the feelings that had arisen in her breast for Philip Templeton? Him, she would see often as he took on the mantle of guardianship to her children.

She should have taken a disgust of him after tonight's revelations. Instead, what was fixed in her mind was the look on his face as he spoke of his loneliness. It had stirred a response in her own breast, for she knew that feeling all too well. No one, on a cursory examination, could have supposed that she and Philip Templeton would have very much in common, but they did. They were both guardians to her children, and they were both lonely. She laughed quietly to herself. That was not sufficient reason to start forming an attachment to the man. She was sure there were plenty of lonely people in this world. It would be foolish to read more into their nascent friendship then what was actually there.

Two days later, bright and early, Philip Templeton presented himself at 11 Upper Belgrave Street, in readiness for their departure. Their cases were quickly stowed in the carriage, and soon they were on their way to the station. Lexie gazed out of the window at the house disappearing from view. It was a grand residence, but she would be glad to return to her unpretentious home in Oxford.

Inside the carriage, the children were unusually quiet, speaking in timid voices. They were still not quite at ease with this gentleman who was to become an important part of their lives. Yesterday, she had sat them down and explained as best she could the situation they were in.

"Is Mr Templeton our new papa?" had asked Emily.

"No, darling," Lexie had responded. "He will be like an uncle, looking out for you and making sure you have all that you need."

"Will we go to live with him?" Edwin had wanted to know.

"No, my love," Lexie had answered patiently. "We will continue to live in our own home, but Mr Templeton, or perhaps you may wish to call him Uncle Philip, will visit us there from time to time."

"You mean like Uncle Ambrose does?" piped up Emily.

Lexie had felt herself flush. "Yes, a little like that," she said. Unbidden came a vision of Philip sneaking into her room at night, the way Ambrose had been wont to do. With a concerted effort, she had chased that errant thought away.

Glancing across at him now, she found his gaze fixed on her, a curious expression on his face. It was as though he were recalling something about her and trying to reconcile it with what he now saw. He nodded slightly on catching her gaze, and smiled. She returned the smile, wondering if he was recalling those wicked words he had whispered into her ear two nights ago. *Would you like that, Lexie? Would you want a man to shower you with his seed? Claim you as his?* Going by her fevered dream that night, and the following, she wanted it very much.

Her breathing quickened, and his sharp gaze did not miss a thing. His eyes fell to her heaving bosom, and when he looked up again, there was a devilish gleam in them. Oh my, but it was warm in this carriage! She licked her lips which had suddenly gone dry. Again, his eyes did not miss the gesture. They flared to a dark sapphire blue.

The spell was broken by Emily, who scrambled onto Lexie's lap and asked in a whisper loud enough for all to hear, "Ma, will you ask Uncle Philip if he will let me draw a picture of him on the train?"

"Why do you not ask him yourself?" replied Lexie, but Emily buried her face shyly in the crook of her mama's neck.

Lexie looked back up at Philip apologetically, but he merely smiled and said, "What a good idea, Emily." The little girl raised her head at this, so he went on, "Do you know that drawing and painting are some of my favourite things to do?"

Emily shook her head in awe. "They are my favourite too," she said.

"Well then, how about we draw each other when we get on the train? I have plenty of sketching paper."

Emily nodded with alacrity. Soon, the dam was broken, and she began chattering with Uncle Philip as if she had known him all her life. A short while later, Edwin too joined in. By the time they reached the station, such was the conviviality of the group that even shy and retiring Fanny had found herself laughing at some remark made by Philip Templeton. And as for Lexie? She passed the remainder of the journey to Oxford alternating between smiling and laughing on the one hand, and on the other feeling hot and aroused whenever Philip directed a fervid look in her direction.

Chapter 10

Philip

Three weeks later

Philip read the letter once more, savouring each word Lexie had written. Three weeks ago, he had escorted her family to their home in Oxford then taken his leave, extracting a promise from her to write to him often and apprise him of their affairs. This she had done, a first letter arriving at Graveley two days later. He had written back that very day.

And so, they had started a back and forth daily correspondence. The letters were informal, candid and dare he say, affectionate? Their arrival had become the highlight of his day. They went a long way towards easing whatever discomfort he might have felt on being the subject of village gossip after the broken engagement with Sarah. Local society had been agog at the news that Sarah had ended her betrothal to him only to run off to America with Benjamin Stanton. He did not go out in public much, and whenever he did, he merely smiled blandly, talking pleasantries and doing his best to ignore the whispers behind his back.

As soon as he returned home, he was at his easel, painting. He had set aside for the meantime his series on transport through the ages, for he had found far better muses. Another sketch, then a painting, had been made of Lexie, this time of her in the carriage with Emily in her lap, shyly burying her face in the crook of her mama's neck. Then he had started a painting of Emily, using the sketches he had drawn on the train. He had tried to bring out her joyful nature and childish curiosity. Next, he planned on a painting of Emily and Edwin, their heads close together as he read her a story.

The thought of being a guardian to these children daunted him less and less each day. No more were they faceless, bothersome children to him, but individuals whose character was beginning to shine through, especially with each letter that came from Lexie, telling him of their daily adventures. There was Edwin, a boy who endeavoured to be the man of the family, precociously stepping into his absent father's shoes. And then there was Emily—angelically pretty, unabashedly joyful yet with a volcanic temper when things did not go her way and a fierce stubbornness to go with it.

Philip picked up the letter and read it a third time, paying special attention to the final paragraphs.

I often think about Tremayne's, especially at night when I am restless. Sometimes I feel a wave of revulsion at the depravity I saw. Other times, I wonder at the freedom of these revellers in setting aside moral conventions. I try to imagine what it must be like to be so free and to take part in such hedonistic revelry. I think of that lady we saw being pleasured by three men. My moral code tells me that lady must be a shameless hussy, but another part thinks what a lucky person she is to have been worshipped by three men at once.

Then of course, I get to thinking about myself. I am after all a member of that club for the next six months. Could I ever do any of the things I witnessed that night? The answer must always be no. And yet… I then wonder about you. In the past, you have been one of those hedonistic revellers. Did those acts turn you into a wicked person? I cannot believe so, for I have seen your kindness to my children and to me.

*My moral certainties, inculcated into me from childhood,
have been eroding over time. Firstly with William's seduction
of me. Some would think that made me a hussy, but I know
myself not to be. Then of course, there was my long affair with
Ambrose. He came to me at night, in secret, and we found joy
in each other's bodies. We also came to love one another deeply
as friends. Did ten years of being a man's mistress make me a
hussy? Society would say yes, of course. And yet once again, I
know myself not to be. What I had with Ambrose was tender
and loving, not shamefully depraved. And out of that union
came Emily. How could I ever regret it?*

*With these examples borne to me of how one can be
incalculably wicked in society's eyes and yet at the same time
remain morally good, I wonder once again about Tremayne's
and about you. I spend a restless night then feeling envious of
that lucky woman who enjoyed such pleasures while I lay each
night alone in my bed.*

Philip set the letter down. "Jenkins," he called out to his
butler. "Send word to the stable to have the carriage saddled. I
leave for Oxford in the next half-hour." He stood then and
hurried up to his chamber, putting together the items he would
need for a short stay in Oxford. At the appointed time, he
stepped out of his house and boarded the carriage.

Over the course of the two-hour journey, his mind went over
the words of Lexie's letter. They were candid words, but they
also held a hidden connotation which he well understood. Lexie
was not only lonely, like him, but she craved the physical touch
of a man. It had been several months of celibacy for her, and for
him. It was past time to do something about it.

He wanted to see the children again of course, and to check
on their wellbeing as befitted his guardian duties. But over and

beyond all this, he wanted to see Lexie again. He was too experienced a man not to know when there were currents of attraction between two people as there were between himself and Lexie. He would be a gentleman, naturally, and not compel her into a liaison with him. However, if as he suspected, she did wish for it, then he would make an unambiguous overture. Neither of them were innocents. There was already between them a level of intimacy, and therefore no need to beat about the bush. Tonight, he wanted to be in Lexie's bed.

Chapter 11

Lexie

Lexie was in her private parlour, engaged in going over her weekly accounts and settling bills, when she heard the doorbell ring. Was she expecting a delivery this day? Frowning, she considered, hearing the vibrating sounds of male voices coming from the hallway.

Then came a knock on the door, followed by her footman, Stibbs, opening it and announcing, "Mr Templeton to see you, madam."

"Thank you, Stibbs," Lexie dismissed him. A moment later, Philip swept into the room. She went to him, holding out her hands with a smile. "Philip, this is a surprise," she said in delight.

"I hope I am not inconveniencing you by arriving unannounced," he replied, keeping hold of her hands.

"Of course not, do come in and take a seat. May I offer you some tea, or perhaps something stronger?" she enquired.

"I think tea would go nicely," he said, finally letting go of her hands and taking a seat. She went quickly to the door and instructed Stibbs to bring a tray of tea. Then, shutting it behind her, she came to sit by Philip, unable to contain the happiness on her face.

"So," she said, hungrily taking in his handsome face and muscular body, "to what do I owe this unexpected pleasure."

"I thought I would stop by and see that you are all well, as befits my duties as a guardian," he explained.

"Of course," she said, feeling mildly disappointed. Why else would he be here? Naturally, he had come to fulfil his role as a guardian. "Edwin has yet to return from school," she went on, "but you may see Emily. She is upstairs with Fanny. I can go fetch her if you wish." She went to stand, but he stopped her with a hand to her arm.

"I will see Edwin and Emily in due course. First, I wish to speak to you." His hand was still on her arm, and she could not but stare at it.

"Of what do you wish to speak?" she breathed.

"Lexie, your letter…" He did not complete the sentence.

She looked up then into his eyes. "What of my letter?"

He held her gaze. "As soon as I read it, I determined to come see you."

She felt her cheeks heat and her heart quicken its beats. "Why is that, Philip?" she ventured to ask.

"Lexie, do not pretend," he said in a deep and gravelly voice that strummed her pulse like a violin. "I am too old for coy games. What if I were to tell you that tonight, I wish to visit your bed, and that I wish to do all sorts of unholy things with you?"

She felt breathless, unable to speak. "What if I were also to tell you," he continued, "that I propose becoming your lover not just tonight, but for the foreseeable future, and perhaps in time become something more than merely your lover? What would you say to that?"

"I—I would say yes," she stammered, her power of speech still compromised.

"That is what I wanted to hear." He stood and pulled her to her feet. "Kiss me, Lexie," he commanded.

She pressed her hands to his chest and did just that. His lips were soft and warm as he accepted and returned her kiss. He did not deepen it, just kept her in the shelter of his arms while they sealed their bargain with the touch of their lips. Looking into her eyes, he promised, "Tonight, I will not be so gentle. But first, we shall have tea and talk, then we shall spend time with the children."

"Yes," she breathed.

"Are your servants discreet? Will they have loose tongues if I stay here tonight? If so, we must come up with some alternative arrangement."

She stopped him with a finger to his lips. "I believe they are discreet," she answered, "though I do not wish to put this discretion to the test. With Ambrose, it was simple, for he stayed in the Stanton house next door, and came in through the back door late at night when everyone was abed. I will send word to Briggs, the butler next door, and ask that a room be prepared for you there. How long do you mean to stay?"

He kissed her finger on his lips. "A few days at least. I want us both to have our fill before I return to Graveley."

"Good," she sighed happily. With Ambrose, it had always been a snatched day, on rare occasions two. He had not been free, like Philip was, to linger. "Tonight at ten o'clock, come out into the gardens and cross over to my house. I shall look out for you."

He laughed. "That sounds rather cloak and dagger to me. I shall go along with it for the time being, but let me tell you, Lexie, that I shall want a more settled arrangement between us. Sneaking about at night is not my way of doing things." He kissed the tip of her nose. "Now, let us sit down again, for I believe your servant shall soon be returning with the tea."

He was right. Not a minute later, there came a knock and Stibbs walked in laden with a tray. They sat, politely talking as if her world had not just spun on its axis. She was to have an affair with Philip Templeton—handsome, experienced, man of the world Philip Templeton. Not just that. He had stated, obliquely, his intention to take their relationship further than being clandestine lovers. Could he mean marriage? He must. She felt a thrill at the knowledge, while at the same time forced herself to be cautious. She was not yet ready to tie herself down to another marriage. What he proposed for now was an affair, and she was happy with that. The future would take care of itself.

These thoughts flitted through her mind as she poured the tea and handed him a cup. They conversed as friends, their earlier contretemps put to one side. Soon, Emily was sent for, and her joy at seeing Philip was something to behold. She rushed to show him her latest pictures, and he looked over them with due care, offering praise and advice. Shortly before lunch, Edwin came home. He too was happy to see Philip, though his delight was more tempered than that of his sister's. Together, they made a merry group as they gathered in the dining room for their meal.

Later that evening, Philip retired to the house next door, and then it was a waiting game until ten o'clock. Lexie bid her children goodnight. She washed her body carefully and brushed her teeth with tooth powder. Offending hairs were plucked away. A few drops of cologne were rubbed over her wrists and throat. Finally, she put on a flimsy silk night rail and covered it with a warm robe. Then, she sat in bed with a book and counted the minutes until it was time.

A little before ten, she put the book to one side, donned soft slippers, and holding a lit oil lamp in one hand, went quietly down the stairs and to the back door. She slipped the lock and drew it open, stepping out into the chill of the night. She did not have long to wait. A moment later, Philip was there. Silently, he followed her up the stairs to her room. The door shut quietly behind him as she set the lamp down at her dressing table. Then, she turned to him. He leaned against the door and watched her carefully.

"Are you sure about this, Lexie?" he asked softly. "There is still time to back out."

She took a deep breath. "I am sure."

"Then, my dear, I am about to make you mine," he stated implacably.

Chapter 12

Philip

Philip prowled towards Lexie who hovered uncertainly beside her dressing table. He came to a stop mere inches from her and stood for a moment, looking fixedly into her expressive eyes. In them, he read need, desire and not a small amount of nerves. She had been mistress to a man before but even so, this was a great step for her to take. It required trust as well as courage to defy society's conventions. He knew and understood.

"Let us establish some rules before we begin," he murmured, still staring into her beautiful eyes.

She nodded.

"Lexie," he went on, "this affair between us will be all about pleasure—yours and mine. I want you to give yourself freely to me and not be afraid. Forget about the rules of proper behaviour. Do not try to be coy. As long as it brings us enjoyment, we can do anything we want." He touched his fingers to the softness of her cheek, holding her gaze. "I plan to do things to you that no man has done before," he said in a throaty voice. "If you do not enjoy them, then simply tell me to stop and I will do so."

"What sort of things do you mean?" she asked breathlessly.

"All sorts of wicked things," he replied with a smile. "I will fuck you in your cunt and in your mouth and in your arsehole." He heard her sharp intake of breath. "I will fuck you in this bedchamber and out of it," he continued, watching her very carefully and taking note of every reaction—the shallow breaths, the flush of her cheeks, the dilation of her eyes.

She licked her lips. "Will you…" She stopped and tried again. "Will you take me to Tremayne's?"

He had thought to put his days at Tremayne's behind him, but in the company of Lexie and in the quest to bring her untold pleasure, he was prepared to venture there again one more time. "If that is what you wish, my dear," he said, "then I will. But let me make one thing clear." His expression hardened. "I will only allow other men to touch you at Tremayne's, at my behest and under my eyes—nowhere else will a man lay a finger on you. No man's cock other than mine will ever enter your cunt, are we clear?" She nodded vigorously. "And again," he went on, "our first rule applies. If you do not enjoy it, then we stop."

"Yes," she murmured. Then a thought came to her. "What about you?" she asked timidly.

He raised a brow in enquiry. Quickly, she added, "Will you be touching other women?"

"Do you want me to?" he asked very softly.

This time, she gave a vigorous shake of her head. He chuckled. "Then I am yours, Lexie, totally and absolutely. Our visit to Tremayne's will be all about you and whatever it is that will please you."

She placed a hand to his chest. "Philip," she breathed. "I want everything you just described, but at the same time, I am fearful."

He covered her hand with his. "Do not be," he said gruffly. "I will protect you always, Lexie. You are safe with me."

"What if…" She sighed. "We can be careful about it of course, but what if I were to become with child? I no longer have the protection of being a married woman."

He put his other hand to her back and drew her gently to him. He felt her face burrow in his chest and was surprised how much he liked having her there. His hold on her tightened. Tucking his chin over her head, he promised, "We will be careful, but if that were to happen, my dear, then I would be quick to put a ring on your finger. I do not want to rush you into anything, but I foresee that we will end up married to each other in any case."

He heard her murmur into his chest, "I have done that before. Rushed to the altar because of a child. It did not turn out well."

"I am not William," he chided gently.

She pulled back to look searchingly into his eyes. "No," she agreed. "You are not William." A pause, then, "However, I am not ready to tie the knot again so soon."

He laughed. "And having just been jilted by my fiancée, I am not ready to become betrothed again so soon."

At this, she smiled and buried her head against his chest once more. Yes indeed, he liked having her there very much. "Then we are in agreement?" he enquired.

"We are in agreement," she confirmed.

"In that case…" He freed his hands and ran them through her hair, cradling her head firmly for his kiss. "I will not be so gentle this time," he warned, before crashing his mouth to hers. Her lips were soft and inviting. It made him all the more eager to plunder them like the most wicked of bandits. He felt her sigh and part her lips to him, allowing his marauding tongue to enter the velvety depths within.

But her mouth was not to be plundered without the launch of a counteroffensive on her part. As he stroked his tongue past her lips, she laid siege to it, sucking it deeply. Next moment, her own tongue was thrusting its way forward in the sweetest of invasions. He moaned as she took possession of his mouth. For a long time, they played this game of cut and thrust, neither coming out the outright victor but both taking their fair share of the spoils. Their mouths and breaths fused, becoming one. He held her tight against him, grinding his swollen cock into her hips. Never before had a simple kiss been so enthralling. He had known she would be sensual, but this—this was beyond anything he had imagined or ever experienced.

"Lexie," he groaned at last. "Oh, Lexie, you are divine." Gently, he pushed her a step back towards the dressing table stool. "Sit there, princess," he ground out breathlessly.

She sank onto the stool obediently, a question in her eyes. In answer, he dropped to his knees before her. Purposefully, he untied the sash of her robe, parting the folds to reveal the delicate silk of her night rail beneath. "So pretty," he purred in approval. He touched a hand to the side of her face, noting the desire in her eyes and the heightened colour in her cheeks. Her lips were pink and swollen from their kisses. She had never looked so beautiful to him as she did in that moment. One day, he promised himself, he would make a painting of the way she looked right now. What lucky quirk of fate had brought this woman into his life? He knew then that he would do all in his power never to let her slip through his fingers.

With deliberate slowness, he trailed his hand down the graceful line of her neck, glorying in the silky soft feel of her skin, then further down until he reached her left breast. He cupped it in the palm of his hand. It was just the right size, fitting perfectly into his hand. He could not resist bringing his free hand to palm her other breast. He squeezed both together, kneading the soft flesh, pleased at her rapid intake of breaths. Next, he ran his thumbs over each nipple, stroking in a circular motion through the thin layer of silk. She moaned her delight— so beautifully responsive.

Leaning forward, he brought his mouth to one puckered tip, drawing it in and sucking the flesh through the silk of her gown. "Oh," she moaned again, her fingers raking through his hair and holding him to her breast in a silent plea for more. He obliged, sucking the pebbled tip some more then giving it a light nip, which elicited a pleased gasp from her. He moved to the other breast, lavishing it with the same attention.

"Philip!" she cried.

He paused and looked up at her.

"Stop teasing me. I need."

"What is it you need?" He slid his hand down the length of her body and brought it to rest on her mound. Through the silk, he pressed his hand firmly to the sensitive flesh beneath. "Is it this?"

"Yes!"

"Then, my darling, that is what you shall have." Carefully, he lifted the ends of her night rail up to her thigh and dipped his hand under the silky material. His fingers stroked the curls at her mound as he instructed, "Part your legs for me."

As she did so, his eyes flew down to get his first look at this most intimate part of her body now bared to his gaze. Nestled under the dark curls were the most delightful pink folds, dewy with her desire. "Lexie, you are perfection," he whispered reverently. Instinctively, his fingers followed his gaze, stroking the moist and delicately soft flesh.

"Oh," she gasped.

With unerring precision, his thumb found the tight little bud of her clitoris and began to rub it gently. All the while, his eyes were fixed on her face, wanting to see her reaction to every touch. Her lips parted as she drew short breaths, her soft brown eyes filled with need. They stared at each other, not looking away for even an instant, as he stroked her sensitive bud over and over.

His other hand now slid to her mound. With infinite care, he inserted an index finger into her wet cunt, his eyes looking to see her reaction. Her lips parted in surprise. "Do you like that?" he asked huskily.

"Yes, I do," she breathed.

"Good," he said in satisfaction. He began to plunge his finger in and out of her, all the while the thumb of his other hand continued with its strokes of her clitoris. Soon, a second finger joined the first, thrusting rhythmically into her. He fucked her rapidly with his fingers, hearing her breath hitch and seeing the desire pool in her eyes. She was close.

He redoubled his efforts, his hands busy stroking and fucking into her. His eyes held hers captive. *"Go on my beauty,"* he thought. *"Give yourself to pleasure."* He did not speak though, letting his eyes do the talking. It was as if she heard. With a soft cry, she reached her climax. He felt the walls of her cunt pulse around his fingers as her eyes shut, giving in to ecstasy. He continued to stroke her until she was spent, then slowly, he withdrew his fingers and held them up. They were coated with the juices of her arousal. He simply had to have a taste. He brought his index finger to his mouth and sucked. "Mmm, delicious," he praised.

Her eyes opened again, watching him as he licked her essence from his fingers with evident enjoyment. "That was amazing," she said in wonder.

He smiled. "That was only the beginning." He brought his hand down to his groin and squeezed his hard length. "My cock is aching to be inside you, sweet Lexie. But first, I think it is time we dispensed with these tiresome clothes." Quickly, he whipped off his robe and threw it carelessly behind him. Beneath it, he was bare. He saw her eyes widen as she took in the sight of his nakedness and the jutting thickness of his cock. "Your turn now, I think," he added.

Timidly, she dispensed with her parted robe. Then it was time to lift the night rail over her head. He helped her to take it off, throwing it in a pile on top of his discarded robe. He continued to kneel at her feet while she sat on the stool, the rounded curves of her body exposed to his hungry gaze. "Oh, Lexie, how beautiful you are," he said admiringly.

"You flatter me, Philip."

He frowned in disapproval. "No, Lexie. I tell only the truth. You are beautiful." His hands traced over the creamy softness of her skin, pausing in their journey to fondle her perfect breasts. "And these titties were made to fit in my hand," he went on. He leaned forward and took a nipple into his mouth, sucking on it lightly. He looked up at her again. "I think," he said consideringly, "that I will fuck you here, on this stool. What do you say to that?"

"I have never made love anywhere but on a bed," she said. "How would we do it?" Her eyes gazed at him in curiosity.

He could not resist dropping a kiss on her soft lips. "Come forward to the edge of this stool and part your legs wide for me," he instructed. "That's my good girl," he praised as she went to do as he asked. Still kneeling on the floor, he took hold of his cock, giving it a few strokes before guiding it to her slick entrance. He pushed in gently an inch or two. "Lean back on your hands, darling, and wrap your legs around me," he said, taking hold of them and crossing them behind him. Then, very slowly, gathering her close, he pushed in deeper, not stopping until he was fully sheathed in her tight heat.

"How does that feel?" he asked, nuzzling the fragrant skin at her throat.

"Strange but good," she breathed in wonder.

He chuckled and promised, "We are going to do all sorts of strange but good things together." He began a series of short thrusts into her. "The best thing about fucking you like this," he continued, "is that I get to worship these glorious titties." So saying, he dipped his head to one taut nipple and sucked it into his mouth.

"Oh!" he heard her gasp. Encouraged, he went on with his very enjoyable task, paying homage to each breast in turn while fucking into her delicious heat. He took his time, varying his strokes into her cunt from quick and shallow to slow and deep. The urge to come was strong, so pleasurable was it to be inside her, but he was experienced and knew, the longer he held off, the greater would be the pleasure for both of them.

At length, he felt the tightening of her passage and quickening of her breaths, signifying that she was close to achieving a second orgasm. He gave one final suck on her breast and released it with a little pop. He looked up into her flushed face. He wanted to see every expression in her eyes as she reached her climax. "Come, Lexie," he urged. "Spend on my cock."

And now he began to plunge into her, deep and hard. "Go on, my girl," he rasped. "Let yourself go." He thought he would drown in the entrancing gaze of her brown eyes. There were no more words after that, just grunts and gasps as they stared at each other and fucked. With each hard thrust of his shaft, his eyes telegraphed the message, *"See me, Lexie. See who is bringing you such pleasure."*

He felt it and saw the moment it happened. Her breath hitched and her eyes rolled up as bliss overtook her. At the same time, he felt the walls of her cunt tighten and pulse around his cock buried deep inside her. She was magnificent in her pleasure. He grunted as he plunged into her, hard and fast, letting her ride out every last moment of her climax. When at last, she sighed and went still, it was his turn.

With a wrench, he pulled out his glistening cock and rose to his feet, pumping it wildly with one tight fist. He rasped out the question he had asked all those weeks ago at Tremayne's. "Do you want me to shower you with my seed, Lexie? Claim you as mine?"

She stared at his cock and his fast pumping hand, too mesmerised to speak.

"Answer me!" he urged, desperation creeping into his voice.

Her eyes flew up, reading the need in his. "Yes," she breathed. "Yes, claim me."

With a hoarse cry, he spurted his release, painting her marvellous breasts with the pearly emission of his seed. He stood over her, out of breath, as he came down from the throes of his passion. Then with two fingers, he swirled the sticky substance of his seed over her skin, as if using a paintbrush on canvas. Of course, he was no wild creature, having to mark a possession with his scent, but all the same, he felt as if he were, in some indelible way, marking her and making her his for posterity. That marriage they spoke of earlier—it would have to come sooner rather than later if he had anything to do with it.

He lifted the two fingers, soaked in his musky essence, and offered them to her. Obediently, she parted her lips and sucked them clean. He gazed at her approvingly, then reached towards the dressing table, taking a folded muslin cloth. He dipped it into the small bowl of scented water and brought it back to wipe her body clean. She watched him, eyes fixed on his actions.

"Speak to me, Lexie," he growled.

"I am speechless," she murmured. "Never before has it been like this."

He felt a surge of gladness. He may not have been her first lover, but he was the first to bring her such joyful experiences. And the last, he promised himself.

Once he was done, he discarded the cloth and held out his hands to her. "Come, darling," he said. "Let us go to bed." Together, they got under the covers and embraced, their naked bodies fitting perfectly to each other. He held her to him, listening to her soft breaths deepen as she slowly slipped into slumber. He kept hold of her, even after she slept, thinking over everything that had occurred between them. Over the years, he had had many lovers, too many to count. He was a jaded rake, he knew, but also one that wanted finally to settle into domestic contentment with a constant companion. This was, after all, why he had proposed to Sarah Cranshaw, and why, when that had fallen through, he had been prepared to endure the forthcoming season to find himself another bride. That plan would need to change. There was only one woman he wanted and that was the one in his arms now.

He sensed that what he had with Lexie was different to all that had come before. He was not sure if he could call it love, at least not yet. He felt though, that there was every indication that in time, it would grow into that elusive emotion. They would give each other that time, he thought, each to get over the hurts of the past and let their feelings grow, let their trust deepen.

There was also, he reminded himself, the matter of her children. Marriage to Lexie would put him in the position of father to them. He did not think Lexie was ready yet to afford him such a privilege, and he certainly was not ready himself to take on such an important role in their lives. Becoming their guardian had been a major step, and one he was slowly accustoming himself to. He already cared greatly for Emily and Edwin. He hoped they too were beginning to care for him. He was not much experienced with children, but he thought they enjoyed his company. In time, he hoped they would grow to accept him as a father, but these things could not be rushed.

Gently, he disengaged himself from Lexie's sleeping embrace and left the bed, searching for his robe. He pulled it on, then approached the bed once more. He stood for a moment, staring down at her, feeling an indescribable tug in the region of his heart. He did not want to leave her. He wished he could stay in bed, falling asleep to the scent of her fragrant skin and the sound of her soft breaths. Maybe one day, he sighed.

Picking up the lamp, he quietly made his way out of the room, clicking the door shut behind him. On silent feet, he followed a path down the stairs and towards the back door of the house. This sneaking about at night would have to be brought to an end, he thought. He was too old for such things. As he went to open the back door, a voice hissed behind him. "Who goes there?"

Turning around, he spied Stibbs, the footman, holding a poker in his hand and looking fierce. "Hush now," Philip admonished. "It is only me."

The footman blinked at him in recognition. "Sir," he whispered, taking a step back. "I thought you were an intruder." He narrowed his eyes then. "You will pardon me for asking, but are you here this late at night by invitation of the mistress of this house?"

Philip regarded him thoughtfully. "If I were to say yes, Stibbs, would that information stay between us, or would it reach the ears of others?"

The footman drew himself up stiffly. He looked to be around fifty. "Sir," he said, "I have served this family faithfully since I was a young man. I have known Mrs Forbes since she was a small child and worked in this household since her marriage to the late Mr Forbes. Never has an indiscreet word passed my mouth in all that time."

Philip wondered if by that, he meant he had known of Lexie's affair with Ambrose Cranshaw all those years and not spoken of it. "Good," he said out loud. "Please keep it that way. What about the rest of the servants here? Can they be trusted to be discreet? I will have you know that from hereon, I shall be a frequent guest of Mrs Forbes both during the day and at night."

"Sir," Stibbs replied. "The housekeeper and cook is my good wife, and I can vouch for her discretion. My daughter, Fanny, serves here as parlour maid. She is a timid little thing and wouldn't speak to a soul, but I shall remind her of her duty in any case."

Philip nodded, pleased that Lexie was served by such loyal retainers. "Very well. Know this, Stibbs. I do not propose to be sneaking in and out of this place any longer after tonight. Tomorrow, my belongings will be moved to a guest room in this house which shall be kept for my use whenever I visit. Naturally, I shall speak of this to Mrs Forbes in the morning and obtain her approval for the plan. But I must again insist on your absolute discretion in this matter. You will be well rewarded, I assure you."

"Sir," the footman said, looking affronted. "I do not require a bribe to serve my mistress faithfully."

Philip smiled. "I am glad to hear it. Nevertheless, you may in time be counting me as your new master, and I am in the habit of paying my servants well—as well as expecting their faithful service in return."

The footman looked nonplussed at this, then nodded once. "Yes, sir," he said finally.

"Goodnight, Stibbs," said Philip, then headed out of the back door into the cold of the night. Shivering, he hurried to the next house promising himself that indeed, this would be the very last night he did such sneaking about at night.

Chapter 13

Lexie

Next morning, Lexie stretched languorously in bed, reliving memories of the night before. Her breasts ached and throbbed from Philip's attention to them, and her sex was sore in all the best of ways. She had a new lover! Oh, what a wicked person she was. And yet, she did not feel so wicked, only deliriously happy.

This was no passing dalliance but a permanent new arrangement. Philip had said, had he not, that he proposed to be her lover for the foreseeable future. He had even talked of marriage. Though it was much too soon to think about such things.

Hearing the sounds of her children running down the stairs, Lexie kicked off the covers and got out of bed. She washed, wiping clean the residue of her lovemaking last night, then dressed. A few minutes later, she strode out of her bedchamber and went downstairs to the dining room, in search of her children.

At the door to the dining room, she halted. Was that a male voice she heard? Not just any male voice, but Philip's. She opened the door quickly and went in. The sight she saw made her pause. Three people sat at the dining table—Philip, Edwin and Emily. All three were conversing happily. Philip was in the process of cutting the food on Emily's plate, slicing up the bread and cold roasted beef into small bites for her.

Lexie blinked in shocked surprise just as Philip glanced in her direction. "Ah, my dear," he said cheerfully. "Here you are.

I was about to send Fanny in search of you. Do come and sit here beside me."

In a daze, she went to the seat he pulled out for her and sat down. She looked across at her children, who seemed unconcerned about her lover's presence at the breakfast table. "Good morning, Edwin, Emily," she murmured.

"Good morning, Mama," they both said.

"Coffee, my dear?" Philip asked solicitously.

She could only nod. She ate her meal, listening to the children's chatter with Philip, responding when addressed but otherwise stunned into silence. She could not, of course, discuss private matters with Philip while her children were there, but as soon as they were gone—Edwin to his studies with the schoolmaster and Emily upstairs with Fanny—she would ask him what he was doing.

Finally, breakfast over and the children gone, she marched into her private parlour, Philip at her heels. As soon as the door shut behind him, she whirled to face him.

"Philip, what on earth do you think you are doing?" she exclaimed.

He stood by the door, arms crossed on his chest and stern-faced. "It is very simple, Lexie," he replied coolly. "You may have played cloak and dagger games in your affair with Ambrose, but I will not live a double life, pretending to all that we are mere friends only to sneak into your bed at night. From now on, we are going to be open and honest about our relationship. I do not propose to advertise it to the world, but within this house, there will be no pretence."

"But what about the servants?" spluttered Lexie. "I cannot have them gossip."

"They won't," stated Philip firmly. "I have already spoken to Stibbs about it." His voice softened then, as he came forward to take her hands in his. "Trust me, Lexie. Have I not promised that you are safe with me?"

Next moment, she was in his arms, and he was kissing her. She accepted the embrace, returned the kisses, but still there was an element of doubt in her mind. Could she have Philip here in her house, openly as her lover? It seemed impossible. But how wonderful it would be not to have to pretend.

As if he sensed her doubts, he drew back and held her gaze. "What is it, darling?" he asked.

She sighed, stroking her hand along his broad chest. "You make it sound so easy, Philip, but what if people found out about us?"

"There is no reason for that to happen," he explained reasonably. "You live a quiet life here, and you are fortunate to have loyal servants who have been clearly instructed about the need for discretion." He dropped a kiss on her lips. "Darling, if there is one thing I have learned in nearly four decades on this earth, it is to be true to myself. Nothing corrodes the soul more than living a lie." He kissed her again. "Perhaps if this were to be a short-term fling between us, then we would be best advised to keep it secret. But that is not the case. I mean to be part of your life for a very long time, Lexie."

She rested her head on his chest, enjoying the comfort of being held like this. "What of the children?" she wondered. "Will they not talk inadvertently and let the matter slip?"

She felt his long exhalation of breath. "Possibly," he conceded. "I do not think Edwin would do so, for he is old enough to act sensibly. As for Emily, all she needs to know is that Uncle Philip is a special friend of the family and that he has been charged with taking care of her, along with her mama. That is no secret, for I am, after all, her legal guardian." He kissed the top of her head. "In any case, I have one very quick way to curb any malicious gossip, should any of this get out to the wider world." She looked up at him, a question in her eyes.

"I mean to put a ring on your finger, Lexie," he said by way of explanation. "Not at once—not until we all have had time to get used to each other. But have no doubt, darling, that is the direction in which we are travelling."

She ought to protest. Had she not told herself this very morning that she was not yet ready to contemplate another marriage? Yes, she ought to protest, but his words and the feeling of being held in his arms were far too comforting to do so. It felt good to be wanted. "Very well," she murmured, burying her face into his wonderfully soothing chest and inhaling his masculine scent.

He cradled her in his arms for some time, then drew back. "Come, Lexie, and let us go fetch Emily. I promised her at breakfast that we will do some sketching together," he said with a warm smile.

"Before that," she admonished, "I will need to do a short lesson with her. Every morning, I teach Emily her letters."

"I should like to see that! May I join you for this lesson?"

She giggled. "You may, sir, though you might find it dull."

"Never," he stated, staring at her. He pulled her then for a rough kiss which left her, and him, breathless. Without another word then, he took her hand and led her upstairs to go find Emily.

Chapter 14

Philip

March 1866, one month later

Philip was busy reading Emily a story when the doorbell rang. He paused, wondering who that could be. Lexie lived a quiet life at her house on St Michael's Street and did not often receive visitors. The little girl, sitting comfortably in his lap, prodded his arm. "Go on, Uncle Philip," she demanded.

He dropped a kiss on the little madam's head and resumed the story. A moment later, there came a knock on the door and Stibbs entered. "Viscount Stanton and Mr Cranshaw to see you, madam," he announced.

Lexie set down her sewing and cast him a worried glance. He looked back at her, smiling reassuringly. There was nothing here to fear. Daniel, Viscount Stanton, was an old friend and neighbour of his who had also frequented Tremayne's, though not for several months since he had left for America. As for Ambrose Cranshaw… well, he was sure that the man would not be pleased to hear that Philip had been appointed guardian of his daughter and that he and Lexie were now lovers, but it could not be helped. He would have to get over whatever resentment he felt on the matter.

Stibbs stepped back to allow the newly arrived guests to enter. Daniel walked in first, a grin on his face. Close behind him was Ambrose, his face also wreathed in a grin. Both men came to an abrupt halt and lost their smiles on catching sight of him—and Emily in his lap.

"Philip," said Daniel with a frown. "I had not expected to see you here."

Before Philip could answer, Emily had jumped down and run to them. "Uncle Ambrose! Uncle Daniel!" she cried, beside herself with excitement.

Daniel lifted her up into his arms and kissed her cheek. "Hello, princess," he smiled. "Missed me?"

She nodded, then suddenly assailed by shyness, buried her face into his neck tie. He cradled her to him, murmuring, "And I have missed you. My, how you have grown, young lady."

She looked up at him then and boasted, "I can read too, Uncle Daniel."

"How about you give Uncle Ambrose a cuddle?" asked Ambrose, holding out his arms for her. She went to him willingly, placing a smacking kiss on his cheek. He rocked his daughter in his arms. "Have you been good?" he asked.

"Very good," she pronounced. "Just ask Mama."

"I will," he smiled, "and I shall also want to hear you read." Over her head, Ambrose cast a murderous look in Philip's direction.

"This is not going to be pleasant," Philip thought to himself. He hardened his expression and stared right back at Ambrose. He was not going to be cowed by this man whose sister had jilted him, causing no end of embarrassment for him.

In the event, it was not Ambrose who spoke first but Daniel. Having already greeted Lexie, he came over to him and bowed. "Philip," he said. "It is good to see you, but I must confess to being perplexed by your presence here."

Philip decided there and then not to beat about the bush. Swiftly, he strode to Lexie's side and put his arm around her shoulder, drawing her to his body in a clear statement of possession. "I am here, Daniel," he drawled, "because Lexie is to become my wife." He squeezed her shoulder in warning.

They might not be officially betrothed yet, but they were as good as engaged.

"What?" This last exclamation came from Ambrose, whose face reddened in fury. "You will do no such thing!"

"Uncle Ambrose, why are you angry at Uncle Philip?" asked a bewildered Emily, before bursting into tears.

"Now look what you have done," muttered Philip in disgust. He stepped towards them, meaning to take hold of Emily and console her, but Lexie was quicker.

"Enough! All of you." She flashed a fierce look at all three men, then took hold of Emily. "Oh darling, don't fret," she soothed her daughter. "Uncle Ambrose isn't angry, just very surprised," she said, giving Ambrose a warning look.

Chastened, Ambrose stroked Emily's hair, saying, "That's right, my dearest. I am not angry, just very, very surprised." These last words were said with a raise of his brow in Philip's direction.

The next few minutes were spent in comforting and petting Emily, who soon stopped crying and begged for her uncles' attention. This, they willingly gave her. Lexie's pointed look to all of them made it clear she would not tolerate any further discussion of the matter in Emily's presence. It was well understood by all. So, it was not until much later, after Edwin had returned from school and they had all finished dinner, and after the children had been put to bed, that the four adults finally found themselves alone in Lexie's parlour.

No sooner had the door closed behind them than Daniel spoke. "Now Lexie, please explain what is going on. We came as soon as Ambrose read your letter, informing him of William's passing. What on earth is all this talk of you marrying Philip?"

Lexie gazed at him helplessly for a moment, and Philip decided it was time for him to intervene. Placing a hand on

Lexie's shoulder, he stated, "It is quite simple, Daniel. Firstly, upon reading William's will, we found out that I had been appointed the children's guardian jointly with Lexie."

"Absolutely not!" cried Ambrose. He stepped towards Philip angrily, but was stopped by Daniel, who placed a heavy hand on his arm.

"We were as shocked about it as you," continued Philip, "but I am afraid there are no two ways about it. I am legally guardian to Edwin and Emily Forbes."

"What about the rest?" enquired Daniel, his mouth set in a thin line.

"The rest is also simple," responded Philip. "Lexie and I became friends, then lovers. And I plan, just as soon as she will let me, to put a ring on her finger."

Now Ambrose directed his angry stare at Lexie. "Have you taken leave of your senses, Lexie? This man is a rake, a reprobate, a corrupter of other men. How could you think of marrying him and letting him live in the same household as our children?"

A rake and a reprobate? Philip would concede to those accusations, though he was a reformed rake now. But a corrupter of men? That was putting it too harshly, unless that is… Ah, now he saw. He had, after all, inducted Daniel into the goings on at Tremayne's. Ambrose must have somehow discovered this fact. Philip opened his mouth to speak, but Lexie was quicker.

"I know very well what manner of a man Philip is, Ambrose, and while he may be all of the things you have mentioned, he is also something else and more." Her voice rose in her passion, and Philip was unable to look away from the emotion flashing through her expressive eyes. "He is the kindest, most generous person I have ever known. He is infinitely patient with both Emily and Edwin. He makes me feel safe, protected and cherished in a way I have never felt before. And, most importantly, he loves me—me and only me." She pointed at herself. "He loves me, and I love him," she stated baldly.

"Oh, darling," said Philip, much moved. Uncaring of their audience, he pulled her into his arms and captured her lips in a long, scorching kiss. He drew back slightly, his lips still close to hers, and wondered out loud, "How did you know? I have not yet declared my feelings."

She huffed. "I knew! You show your feelings every day, my love, without the need for words."

"But sometimes, there is a need to say them," he smiled, kissing her sweet lips again. "Lexie, darling, I love you."

"And I love you."

There was a clearing of a throat. The spell broken, they looked towards the two men watching them with differing expressions on their faces—Daniel, with amusement and surprise, Ambrose, with anger and disdain.

Lexie directed her words at her erstwhile lover. "Ambrose, I know this comes as a shock to you, and you will need time to accustom yourself to this news. But you will have to, for I am going to marry Philip and he is going to be a father to our children." Ambrose clenched his fists at this, so she went on quickly. "That does not take away from the fact that the children love you too, very much. And if you think on it in a calm, considered manner, then you will realise that with my marriage to Philip, you will get to see the children more often, as we will become neighbours. Instead of your weekly visits, you will get to see them every day if you wish."

Daniel placed a calming hand on Ambrose's shoulder. "What Lexie says makes sense," he mused. "Living at Graveley, they will be less than a mile distant from your home."

Ambrose ground his teeth. "Yes, but they will be living in his home!" He cast a seething glance at Philip.

"I am not the devil incarnate, you know," responded Philip mildly. "They will be safe, happy and well cared for in my home, of that you have my word."

Ambrose huffed disbelievingly. It would take more than a few promised words to ease his misgivings, this much was clear. Philip sighed to himself. There was nothing more he could do about it now. It seemed Daniel had come to the same conclusion. Speaking softly to his friend, he said, "Come Ambrose, let us take our leave and reflect on the matter this evening." Looking towards Lexie and Philip, he added, "Congratulations on your engagement. I wish you both happy." With that last statement, he led Ambrose out of the room, and then out to the neighbouring house where they were staying.

Lexie burrowed into Philip's arms. "Thank the Lord that is over," she said, sounding relieved. "Do you think Ambrose will come round?" she asked a trifle anxiously.

"He will have to," responded Philip calmly. "He does not have much choice in the matter. Now, darling, let us go up to bed. I feel the need to ravish you." He took her hand and led her upstairs where he did, indeed, ravish her most deliciously.

Epilogue

Lexie

June 1866, three months later

"Are you ready, darling?" asked Philip worriedly. "You know it is not too late to back out if you have changed your mind." They were at Tremayne's and about to enter the room of pleasure for the first time since that occasion five months previously when she had walked in there, curious to find out what it was. Philip had asked this same question several times already tonight, and each time, her answer was the same.

"I am ready."

With one final, concerned look, Philip opened the door to the room of pleasure and ushered her inside. As before, they found themselves in a dimly lit room filled with naked persons cavorting hedonistically with one another. They stood for a moment, taking in the sight of this depravity. Then, a maid approached them. "May I undress you, sir?" she asked. At Philip's nod, she proceeded to do so, folding his clothes neatly and putting them away. Next, she came to Lexie and undressed her too.

A moment later, she was naked. Lexie stood, awash with fear, shame and no small amount of excitement. This was it. There was no going back to her sedate, respectable existence after tonight. This was Lexie stepping out of the conventions of society, being wild and free. Philip took her hand and squeezed it reassuringly. She was not alone. In this adventure, Philip was with her. He would look out for her and keep her safe. There was nothing to fear when he was by her side. "Ready?" he whispered.

"Yes."

Together, they stepped forward into the room. A buxom brunette approached them, and Lexie recognised her. It was Cleo, the lady she had met the last time she had visited Tremayne's. "Philip!" That lady cried. "How glad I am to see you. Will you share some fun with us?"

But Philip shook his head. "I am afraid not, Cleo. I am here for Lexie's pleasure only. I belong to her now, you see, and I am not to touch any lady but her."

Cleo's face fell. "Such a shame." With a shrug, she walked away, pulling her husband along with her.

Philip turned to his fiancée, soon to be his wife—for the wedding was to take place in two days' time. "Take a good look around this room, darling, and tell me if you see any man that catches your attention."

Now it was her turn to squeeze his hand. That last question had not been an easy one for him, she knew. Before coming tonight, they had talked extensively about it. Philip had told her, in no uncertain terms, how possessive and jealous he felt about any man laying a finger on her. At the same time, he understood very well the intoxicating excitement of being desired and pleasured by multiple partners. Had he not had many years of doing this himself? He would not deny her this experience. He had also confessed something else—that despite his jealousy, he thought he would find the sight of her pleasure intensely arousing and that a part of him would enjoy showing her off to these other men. They would get to see and touch her for a few hours only while he, Philip, had the privilege of doing so every night.

Hand in hand, they stood and looked around the room. "Over there," said Lexie, nodding her head toward a tall, broad man with dark hair and eyes. Philip tracked her gaze to the man and nodded. "Do you know him?" asked Lexie.

"His name is Justin Brentley. Come with me, Lexie, and let me do the talking."

Together, they walked toward Justin, who was busy having his cock sucked enthusiastically by a blonde-haired vixen. As they approached, he ran his eyes over Lexie's curves then back to her face. His own broke out into a grin, showing strong white teeth. "Well, well," he said. "What have we here?"

"Brentley, this is Lexie, soon to be my wife. She is here for her pleasure," said Philip.

"Aren't we all?" mocked Justin.

Philip turned to Lexie. "Take a good look at this man, darling. Would you like him to pleasure you?"

Lexie felt her heart pound in excitement and fear. This man looked brutish and wild and totally sinful. "Yes," she breathed, holding on tight to Philip's hand.

"Step closer, Lexie, and let him fondle your beautiful titties," said Philip gruffly. Together, they stepped even closer, going around the blonde who was still busy worshipping the man's cock.

With eyes that gleamed, Justin reached out his hand and palmed her breast. She let out a sharp breath. Another man was fondling her, and Philip was watching. Her eyes flew to the man she loved. He smiled and bent to kiss her lips. "It's alright, my darling. Enjoy yourself."

The hand at her breast pinched her nipple. She felt a corresponding throb in her core below. "Very pretty," drawled Justin. He brought a hand to squeeze the other breast, rubbing his thumbs over her nipples, which stood proudly to attention. "And very responsive," he added approvingly. "Come closer, pretty Lexie. I won't bite." He chuckled very darkly and added, "At least not too hard."

Her hand still held in Philip's, she came closer to Justin until their faces were only inches apart. He leaned forward and brushed his lips to hers. Good gracious! This man had his hands on her breasts and his lips on hers. And oh, wicked hussy that she was, it aroused her greatly.

"Go on, darling. You may kiss him," said Philip gently beside her. She cast him a quick look, seeking reassurance. He smiled, though she detected a burning flare in his eyes. Jealousy? Arousal? Maybe a little of both.

She turned to Justin with a shy smile. He flashed a grin at her. "Philip, you lucky bastard," he said, before bringing his mouth to capture hers. This time, his kiss was not light or gentle. It was demanding, aggressive even. This man was taking what he wanted from her, and right this moment, he commanded her, through the whip of his tongue, to part her lips for him. This she did on a soft sigh, allowing him to lick his way into her mouth, to nip—none too gently—and then to suck the sting away. He tasted different and smelled different to Philip. It was not unpleasant at all, just different. And wanton hussy that she was, she revelled in this exciting adventure being played out.

As they kissed, his hands kneaded her breasts and pleasured her erect nipples. She felt a rush of wetness drip down from her core. As if he felt it too, Philip said beside her, addressing Justin, "Touch her cunt, Brentley. Is she as wet as I think she is?"

Immediately, one of Justin's questing hands dropped from her breast and slid down to the curls on her mound, brushing through them briefly before seeking the moist flesh below. A finger stroked along her cunt and came back up, soaked with her juices. His mouth still ravishing her own, Justin held up his hand for Philip to see. "Taste her!" rasped Philip.

With one last tug of his tongue, Justin released her mouth, only to suck in his finger, wet with her essence. He looked at Philip then. "She tastes good," he confirmed.

By now, the blonde at his cock, seeing Justin's distraction, had moved along to seek pleasure elsewhere. He was free to lavish all his attention on Lexie.

Philip looked at her. "Darling, would you like Brentley to eat your cunt?"

She nodded, speech impossible at this moment in time. At her acquiescence, Philip led her to a wide couch propped up with several pillows. He settled her on one end and drew open her legs, baring the most intimate part of her body to Justin's avid gaze. "Oh, she is a beauty," he grunted.

As Justin dropped to his knees on the floor before her, Philip issued a challenge. "Bring her to orgasm within two minutes, Brentley, and I will allow you to fuck her arsehole." Philip's eyes stared directly into hers, looking for any sign of disagreement. She simply nodded. They had fucked like this several times at home, and while it had been a little painful at first, she had ended up enjoying it greatly. Philip now addressed her, "While he fucks your arse, darling, I think Grayson will be next to eat your cunt." He nodded towards another man who had been silently watching the proceedings and stroking his engorged cock.

Her eyes met Grayson's, a fair-haired man with a lean, wiry physique. He smiled gently, though desire was evident on his face. She smiled back, feeling her arousal grow. Then all thought of Grayson was wiped from her mind as Justin's tongue licked a long lap of her cunt. "Ah," she cried, her body twitching in surprise.

"Stay still, Lexie," Philip admonished sharply. He put his hands to her legs, holding her open for Justin's delectation. Exchanging glances with the man, he said throatily, "Your two minutes start now." Justin set to work immediately, lapping at her cunt with long strokes of his tongue. She cried out again, held in place by Philip's strong hands, unable to evade the intense sensation of being ravished by that tongue. And if that wasn't enough, Philip then rasped, "Grayson, come and eat her titties." The man did not need to be asked twice. Soon, she felt the suction of his mouth on her sensitive nipple, while his hand played with the other. All the while, Philip watched, directing the proceedings to his, and her, satisfaction.

Lexie searched Philip with her eyes. "Philip, I—I..." but she could not go on. A moan escaped her as her core quivered in a powerful climax. Throughout it all, Philip held her gaze, his own eyes burning fiery bright.

"Good girl," he praised, his voice hoarse with need.

Justin raised his head and smirked, his lips wet with her juices, "Well under two minutes," he gloated.

"Lexie, darling," Philip instructed crisply. "Kiss Brentley and taste yourself on him."

With a swagger, Justin rose to his feet and strode over to her. He leaned down to her in an open-mouthed kiss. Her tongue brushed against his, tasting him, tasting herself. She wanted more. With a newfound confidence, she clasped his head in her hands and held him to her while she kissed him hungrily. Her attention was on Justin's kiss, but it was also on Philip. Instinctively, she knew where he was and felt his gaze observing this torrid kiss. Was it driving him wild with jealousy? And why did this arouse her so?

Eventually, she released Justin from her clutches and he drew back, wicked desire gleaming in his eyes. Beside her, Philip growled softly, "Will you let him fuck your arse, Lexie?"

She looked into Justin's darkly gleaming eyes. "Yes," she said decisively.

"Good choice," approved Justin. "Turn around, Lexie, and present your arse to me. I shall need to prepare you for my great cock."

At Philip's nod, she did as she was bid, holding herself on her hands and knees. Philip handed Justin a bottle of oil. He quickly poured some drops onto his palm and stroked his greased fingers along her back hole. At his touch, she shivered in excitement. "That's it, Brentley," she heard Philip say. "Keep stroking her there. She likes it." Justin's fingers circled her hole over and over, making her moan out loud.

"Oh, yes, she likes it very much," purred Philip. He ran a gentling hand down her back. Just then, Justin's finger paused at her hole and began to burrow inside.

"Philip!" cried Lexie.

"Yes, darling. You can take it."

She gasped as Justin's finger began to plunge in and out stretching her for his cock. "Fuck her with two," barked Philip. Soon, the first finger was joined by a second, plunging rapidly into her. "More oil." Justin paused and accepted more drops of oil on his fingers. Then the plunging began again, this time a little deeper. "Three fingers." Justin stopped only long enough to slowly insert a third finger into her.

"Philip," moaned Lexie.

"Can you take it, darling?"

"Yes," she moaned. Justin's three fingers resumed their work, plunging and stretching, getting her ready for what was to come. Lexie closed her eyes and focused on the sensation of those three fingers burrowing in and out of her. There was no pain, only a strange feeling of fullness.

"She's ready." Upon Philip's pronouncement, the fingers stilled and withdrew.

"How do you want me to take her?" enquired Justin.

"Lexie, darling, come off the couch and let Brentley take your place," said Philip in response.

On shaky legs, she shifted her body to stand, allowing Justin to lie on the couch in her place. Her gaze fell on his cock. It was thick and long, though not as long as Philip's. As if reading her thoughts, Philip grunted. "You can take him." Then, he was all business. "Come here, Lexie, and present your arse to Brentley. That's it, my girl, bring your leg over here." Philip helped her straddle Justin with her back to his chest. She felt Philip take hold of Justin's cock and position it at her entrance. "Lower yourself onto it, darling," he encouraged.

Slowly, she brought her body down, feeling Justin's cock spear inside her. She moaned, feeling a shaft of pain, and stopped. "Relax your body," murmured Philip. "Try again, slowly." She began to lower herself down again, letting Justin's fat cock fill her. "That's it, darling. Only a little more." She pushed down again until she had taken all of Justin's length. "Oh, what a good girl you are," praised Philip. "Lean back and rest against Brentley's chest."

Justin's arms came around her, holding her to him. His cock rested inside her arse, but he did not move. "You feel good, Lexie girl," he whispered gruffly.

Hearing this, Philip snapped sharply. "You are not allowed to come until I say so, Brentley."

The man huffed in amusement. "I had guessed as much."

Philip touched her cheek gently. "How do you feel?"

She smiled back weakly. "Strange but good."

He chuckled. "That's good. Are you ready for Grayson to eat your cunt now. The man is getting impatient to taste you."

She looked over Philip's shoulder to where Grayson stood, stroking his cock. "Yes," she breathed.

Once again, Philip parted her legs, baring her cunt to another man's gaze. "Eat your fill, Grayson, but she will not suck on your cock unless you make her climax."

Grayson grinned. "Your challenge is accepted," he said on a laugh. Next moment, he had brought his mouth to her cunt and begun to caress her with his tongue.

Imprisoned by Justin's cock in her arse and Philip's hands on her legs, she could not move, could not do anything except feel the touch of Grayson's marauding tongue. Justin's hands were at her breasts, kneading and pinching. And as ever, Philip's fiery gaze tracked every movement, every reaction. After a while, Philip barked another order. "Put two fingers inside her cunt and fuck her with them." Grayson did as instructed, fucking her in a quick rhythm with his fingers while his tongue fluttered back and forth over her sensitive nub.

"Arh!" cried Lexie, overcome with sensation.

"Go on, darling, let yourself go," urged Philip.

Grayson's tongue and fingers picked up speed, so did Justin's fingers pinching her nipples. She could felt her orgasm rise up like a raging maelstrom. On and on it grew until finally, she cried out as it reached its final crescendo.

"Ah, Philip! Philip!"

"Yes, darling. Clever Lexie. You did so well." Philip's voice was thick with desire.

Her panting breaths slowed as she came back to her senses. Philip looked into her eyes, dazed still with the force of her last orgasm. "Will you reward Grayson, darling, with a suck of his cock?"

She nodded as Grayson approached her, his cock standing to attention. It was not too large, but well formed. With a smile, he came to stand at her side, while Philip gazed on from the other. "Put him in your mouth, darling."

Gently, Grayson nudged her lips with his hard length. She parted them and accepted his offering. He slipped inside until about half his length was buried in her mouth. "You can take more," gritted Philip. "Open your mouth wider and relax your throat."

With an effort, she did as instructed. Slowly, Grayson pushed deeper into her mouth until he could go no further.

"Listen to me, Lexie. You are going to let Grayson fuck your mouth. Just stay still and relaxed, let him do the work." Then, addressing the man who had his cock down her throat, he said, "You have two minutes, Grayson, nothing more."

With a grimace, Grayson nodded and began to fuck her mouth. She felt him hit the back of her throat. Tears welled in her eyes. It was dreadfully uncomfortable, yet at once wonderfully arousing. She was the vessel for his pleasure. She held the power. And as Philip watched on with the eyes of a hawk, she knew that he would praise her for a job well done if she could bring Grayson to a climax. Would he fill her mouth with his seed? Her mind was too hazy to think. All she could do was feel as Grayson grunted into her and Justin filled her back hole, shifting slightly every so often to remind her of his presence inside her.

"One minute," Philip warned.

Grayson renewed his efforts, grunting like a wild animal as he fucked his cock into her mouth. Tears rolled down her cheek, as she took every thrust, looking up into Grayson's frantic face and knowing she was the reason for his wild loss of control. And suddenly, on a loud groan, he gushed his spend into her mouth. "Swallow it," barked Philip.

With an effort, she gulped it down, its musky tang filling her mouth as Grayson pulled his spent cock out. And then Philip was there, straddling her and looking fierce as he crashed his mouth to hers and licked the remnants of Grayson's seed clean. He kissed her over and over, telling her what a good, clever girl she was, and how proud he was. He licked the tears from her face and kissed her again. "I love you, Lexie."

"I love you too," she sobbed, unable to contain her emotion. He gentled her with more kisses, then finally raised his head to look into her eyes.

"Darling, do you have the strength for one more bout. I would like to put my cock into your cunt, and then have us both fuck you at once. Do you think you can take it, sweet Lexie?"

She gazed trustingly at him and nodded. Behind her, she felt Justin kiss the back of her neck, then whisper into her ear, "You are magnificent, Lexie. Let us fuck you now." She nodded again.

Philip took his swollen cock and guided it to her entrance. With his eyes fixed on hers, he pushed in slowly. It was a very tight fit, with Justin's cock already taking so much space. Using small, shallow strokes, he burrowed deeper and deeper into her cunt until finally, she had taken his entire length. She had never felt so full. Speech was impossible, so she let her eyes do the talking, staring at Philip with all the need and emotion she felt. He grimaced, half in pain, and bit out. "You feel so good, Lexie. I shan't last very long."

Then, both Philip and Justin started to fuck her. They took it in turns, one man thrusting then retreating while the other man plunged in. They worked in tandem, finding a rhythm together. She heard their groans of agony or ecstasy—it was a fine line between the two. And as they filled her with their cocks, she marvelled at the sensation of being taken by two strong and virile men. Sweat poured down their brows as they groaned and grunted, their pleasure so exquisite that they lost themselves in it, taking her along for the ride to Valhalla.

She felt their pleasure grow and knew exactly when it was that their control snapped. No longer were they in rhythm. They simply bucked and cried out loud as they reached their blessed release, each showering her with their seed. Philip roared as he spent himself in her, and she held him tight. Her Philip. Her love. The generous man that had gifted her with this incredible experience, even at a cost to himself. He collapsed atop her, breathing heavily and she saw there were tears in his brilliant blue eyes. He brought his forehead to hers and communed with her for a few silent moments.

Then, with infinite gentleness, he withdrew his cock from her cunt and lifted her off Justin, cradling her in his arms. With long strides, he took her to a side room with towels and jugs of water. Tenderly, he bathed her, cleaning off every residue of sex. When he was done, he held her, stroking his hands down her back and arms. She trembled, experiencing a delayed reaction to all that had been done. He understood and gentled her with his kisses until her trembling stopped.

They heard a sound next to them and turned to see Justin dip a cloth in the water he had poured into a basin, and begin to clean himself. He smiled at them. "That was extraordinarily good," he said. "Thank you for allowing me to share in your pleasure tonight."

She smiled shyly, unable to formulate any words. Philip nodded curtly. "Thank you, Brentley, for helping Lexie achieve such pleasure, but I must tell you, it will not happen again. This was the one and only time that we shall visit Tremayne's. The day after tomorrow, we are to marry, and then there will be no other man but me to touch my wife."

Justin gave a wry smile. "Then I am fortunate indeed to have been afforded this chance," he said. "May I wish you both happy nuptials." With that, he inclined his head in a gesture of goodbye and left them.

Philip gazed tenderly at Lexie. "Darling, are you ready to get dressed? I am eager to take you home."

She sighed. "Yes, let us get dressed and go."

Without a word, they left the room to fetch their clothes. Once dressed, they left Tremayne's hand in hand, climbing into the carriage that waited for them outside. Although it was not a long walk to Philip's house, where they were all staying, she was too weary and sore for it. As the carriage began its leisurely journey, Lexie laid her head on Philip's shoulder. "Thank you," she said softly.

"I would do anything for you, my darling," he replied, "but please, do not ask me to share you with others ever again."

She laughed gently. "I promise I will not. Once was more than enough, and I believe I have made enough memories tonight to last me a lifetime."

He tightened his hold on her. "Good." They spoke no more after that as the carriage took them home. Once in their bedchamber, they undressed, throwing their clothes carelessly to one side, and got into bed, reaching for each other's comforting embrace. They said goodnight and fell asleep, their last thought as both drifted into slumber, was that two nights hence, they would sleep as man and wife.

Afterword

Dear reader,

I hoped you enjoyed this spin-off novella from **The Stanton Legacy** series. You may also be interested to read another novella linked to this series, **Miss Stanton Meets her Match**, which tells the story of Isabella Stanton in an age-gap, enemies-to-lovers romance with her tenant at Netherwick Hall.

Please also consider subscribing to my newsletter on **mmwakeford.substack.com** to get latest authorly news, book recommendations and freebies.

May I ask you for a small favour?

Reviews are the life blood of independent authors. Please could you help spread the word about this book by submitting a review on Amazon, Goodreads or any other book reader platform. Thank you!

M.M. Wakeford

About the author

M.M. Wakeford lives with her husband and son in a London terraced house that gathers dust while she loses herself in her writing. A lifelong reader of romantic novels, she writes in many genres including contemporary, sci-fi and historical romance. All her stories strive to capture that heady feeling of falling in love, with authentic characters whose journey to a happily ever after is lined with dilemmas to overcome. If you're looking for a page turning romance with high emotion and a good dose of spice, you've come to the right place.

Also by this author

MISS STANTON MEETS HER MATCH

A Stanton Legacy Novella
An Age-Gap, Enemies-to-Lovers Historical Romance

Isabella Stanton had determined from an early age that the fact of having been born female would not stand in the way of her doing what she desired. Having inherited a substantial estate from her grandfather, she insisted on taking an active role in managing her affairs, including the tenancy of Netherwick Hall, the magnificent mansion on her estate.

Enter Silas Wilson, her new tenant, a widower from Manchester with two young children. He was everything that she disliked—brash, ill-mannered and a man who had made his fortune in manufacturing, no doubt on the exploitation of the poor workers in his factories. Isabella despised him on sight.

She consoled herself with the knowledge that she would not have to see him again at all once he took residency of Netherwick Hall. In this assessment, she was to be proved entirely wrong...

Author's note: This historical novella is a steamy age-gap, enemies-to-lovers romance with spin off characters from The Stanton Legacy series. You do not have to have read the other books in the series to enjoy this novella, as it can be read as a standalone, though your enjoyment of it will be enhanced if you are familiar with the rest of the timelines and characters.

THE VISCOUNT'S SCANDALOUS AFFAIR

Book 1 – The Stanton Legacy

"Why not have a short dalliance with me? In the cold desert of my spinsterhood, I assure you I will not treasure my virtue half as much as the memories of sensual pleasures with you."

Life has not been kind to Charlotte Harding. Orphaned, impoverished and plain-looking, she depends on the charity of relatives who take her in when she has nowhere else to go. In their London home, she meets the rich and handsome Viscount Stanton who is promised to the beautiful heiress, Miss Powell. Charlotte is smitten with him on first sight, but the Viscount barely notices her except to note her unprepossessing looks and shabby dress.

One night at a society ball, Charlotte accidentally witnesses a secret tryst between the viscount and his mistress - and is unfortunately discovered. Her silence is bought with an unforgettable kiss that leaves Charlotte yearning for more. So when she learns that the viscount has ended his relationship with his mistress, Charlotte seizes the opportunity to make him a scandalous offer - a short, discreet affair in return for memories to treasure in her spinsterhood.

Author's note: The Viscount's Scandalous Affair is a historical romance written in a homage to Jane Austen and Georgette Heyer, with a dose of spice. It features an illicit affair between two unlikely lovers whose emotional and bumpy journey into love ends in a happily ever after.

What people say about The Viscount's Scandalous Affair

"A beautiful story… and the ending was perfection." **Goodreads review**

"Excellent book to curl up with and enjoy. What a way to start a new series. Would strongly recommend." **Goodreads review**

"A stunning read and a great story… compelling and very steamy." **Goodreads review**

"Love this book! Please add this to your TBR lists. This book was explosive from the first chapter and left me wanting more. Great book and a great choice." **Goodreads review**

"An amazing regency romance where you'll feel all the emotions. A mix of twists, forgiveness, angst, steam, drama, love and a second chance at life. So beautifully written." **Di – Amazon review**

"It's hard not to fall in love with Charlotte… This was a charming book and I loved every second of it." **Ashleigh – Goodreads review**

"This book has it all… hold on to your pantalettes! Very raw and scandalous. There is a happy ever after so dive in with your heart open and you won't be disappointed!" **Janine – Amazon review**

THE VIXEN'S UNLIKELY MARRIAGE
Book 2 – The Stanton Legacy

"No, no, we cannot marry. That is absurd."

Grace Stanton is beautiful, vivacious and no innocent when it comes to men. Her carefree, happy life is disrupted when her family is summoned to the bedside of her grandfather, the dying Earl of Stanton, in England. There, circumstances force her into a marriage with the last person she ever thought to marry—Benedict Sedgwick, the newly appointed parish curate who wears threadbare clothes and blushes in the presence of women.

For Benedict, it is infatuation at first sight when he meets Grace Stanton, but he knows that the wealthy beauty is well out of his reach. That is until one day, she comes knocking at his door asking for help, and he cannot help but propose marriage as a way out of her dilemma.

Can a poor, inexperienced and ordinary looking curate win Grace's heart when she yearns for a dashing man of the world, someone like her new neighbour, the handsome Mr Templeton?

Author's note: This is a sweet, steamy and dramatic historical romance set in Victorian England featuring a marriage of convenience between two unlikely characters, a beautiful vixen and a virtuous clergyman, who nevertheless find themselves falling in love.

What people say about The Vixen's Unlikely Marriage:

"Would absolutely give this story more than 5 star rating if I could... a real page turner that you can't stop reading till you're done."
Amazon review

"A delight to read! The story of Benedict and Gracie is an unforgettable tale of love, devotion, daring, sacrifice, believing in miracles, and that there is no limit to what one will do to save the life of one's beloved." **Amazon review**

"Benedict is such a wonderful character – I enjoyed watching him transform from a blushing, stammering shy guy into a supportive and caring partner, willing to do ANYTHING for his wife... Very satisfying all around!" **Amazon review**

"This is a fantastic sci-fi romance... I loved the characters and I highly recommend this book." **Amazon review**

"Very steamy and hot, with a virgin, shy MMC who must learn to please a sexually experienced wife." **Goodreads review**

"I found myself totally immersed in the plot straight away and it kept me hooked right until the end." **Goodreads review**

KRANTOR'S MATE

One day, on a planet far from Earth, I meet my fated mate. The only problem is, he's in love with someone else.

Martha has enrolled on a six-month exchange program to the planet Ven, whose people have recently made first contact with Earth. Newly single and broke, Martha looks forward to this once-in-a-lifetime opportunity to find out more about the Venorians, an intriguing humanoid race of massive bronze-skinned people.

As the son and heir of the Kran, planet Ven's ruler, Krantor has four somars—men who are his lifelong bodyguards and companions. He loves them all dearly, but one of them, Prilor, he loves best of all. Krantor knows he's destined to meet his fated mate one day, but it's Prilor he wants to spend his days and nights with. And he certainly hadn't banked on his fated mate being a human!

Will Martha give up her life on Earth for a fated mate who already loves another? And what of the feelings she has developed for Shanbri, another of Krantor's somars?

Author's note: this is a standalone sci-fi romance with steam and spice aplenty, featuring FM, MM, and MFM relationships, and a guaranteed HEA for all.

What people say about Krantor's Mate:

"What a phenomenal read. The worlds, culture, and species created were diverse and detailed… I went on such an emotional ride with this book." **Amazon review**

"I found this an interesting and original approach to the reverse harem and fated mate tropes... Thought-provoking and provocative, with high heat throughout." **Amazon review**

"M.M. Wakeford offers a completely new take on fated mates. With all the expectations that are set with a trope, the author blows it out of the water with her fabulous storytelling." **Amazon review**

"This is a fantastic sci-fi romance... I loved the characters and I highly recommend this book." **Amazon review**

"Great world building... Lots of yummy steamy scenes to keep me happy, too." **Amazon review**

www.ingramcontent.com/pod-product-compliance
Lightning Source LLC
Chambersburg PA
CBHW070405200726
48294CB00003B/1106